A STROKE OF BAD LUCK

OTHER TITLES BY DIANE JANES

FICTION

The Pull of the Moon
Why Don't You Come for Me?
Swimming in the Shadows
Stick or Twist
The Magic Chair Murder
The Poisoned Chalice Murder

NON-FICTION

Edwardian Murder:
Ightham & the Morpeth Train Robbery
Poisonous Lies: The Croydon Arsenic Mystery
The Case of the Poisoned Partridge
Death at Wolf's Nick: The Killing of Evelyn Foster

A
STROKE OF
BAD LUCK

DIANE JANES

Matador
9 Priory Business Park,
Wistow Road, Kibworth Beauchamp,
Leicestershire. LE8 0RX
Tel: 0116 279 2299
Email: books@troubador.co.uk
Web: www.troubador.co.uk/matador
Twitter: @matadorbooks

ISBN 978 1789017 762

British Library Cataloguing in Publication Data.
A catalogue record for this book is available from the British Library.

Printed and bound in the UK by TJ International, Padstow, Cornwall
Typeset in 12pt Adobe Jenson Pro by Troubador Publishing Ltd, Leicester, UK

Matador is an imprint of Troubador Publishing Ltd

In memory of
Neville Finnemore
1926-2003

CHAPTER ONE

Friday 5 January 1934
His Majesty's Prison, Armley, Yorkshire

As Albert Henshaw paused to unlock the final set of gates, he stole another quick glance at the young woman who was following him. He could see from the flush in her cheeks that she was aware of the curiosity she was generating among the warders, and that she did not welcome it; pretending not to notice the sidelong glances and occasional blatant stares from the men who unlocked each set of doors to admit her, then locked them again when she was safely through.

When he himself had opened the final set of gates, then stepped aside in order that she should precede him, she acknowledged the gesture with the briefest of nods. She was a proper lady all right. No doubt her father had laid out good money, in order that she should be schooled to walk straight and talk proper. Very neatly turned out too, thick tweed coat, brown stockings and sensible brogues – those fashionable little heels that were so popular just now, were no good with the pavements so icy – not but what she wouldn't have come by motor car – she wasn't the sort you'd see on the tram. Her hair was all but hidden under a mustard coloured hat with a green and brown band. Nothing fancy, but made of good quality stuff – a hat that would have cost a working man his week's wages, Albert guessed.

'Not far now, miss.' He had half hoped to initiate some sort of conversation, but she just nodded again, tight lipped. Not being snooty, he decided. Most probably nervous. The forbidding atmosphere of the institution was bearing down on her. The smells, the noises, the metallic clatter and clang of gates and keys, which did not quite obliterate the sound of their footfalls, his the sturdy thump of a good strong pair of boots, hers a dainty feminine pitter-pat.

A different class of visitor to the norm. Alone too. He wondered whether the young woman's father knew that she had come. A big part of him said that Armley Jail was no place for a well brought up young woman. He wouldn't let his Mabel come visiting here, nor their two girls when they were old enough, neither. They might not talk posh like this young lady, but they were respectable and that's a fact. He would have liked Mabel's opinion of the unusual visitor, but he had been warned to say nothing about her to anyone outside. Instructions had come from the governor himself that there must be no loose talk, for fear of something about it appearing in the newspapers.

Well quite! What would the general public make of the news that a man convicted of murder was being visited by the victim's sister? By rights the execution should have been tomorrow, but then word had come through that the condemned man was to be allowed an appeal. Ernest Brown wanted to see whether three judges down in London would have different ideas to a dozen Yorkshiremen, good and true, and in the meantime had come this letter from Miss Florence Morton, sister of the deceased, seeking permission to visit the condemned man, if you please. Albert Henshaw thought it distinctly irregular to say the least, but since Brown himself had raised no objection, there had apparently been nothing in the prison regulations to prevent it.

Naturally he could see why the governor would be concerned about the papers getting hold of it. Rumours of a visit from a member of the victim's family might set all kinds of hares running. There was always a bleeding heart minority who seized on the least little thing to protest that a condemned man was innocent after all, or if not innocent then subject to some sort of extenuating circumstances, or if all else failed, to claim that the fellow hadn't known what he was doing at the time. Abolitionists at heart of course. Well thankfully they didn't run the country and those that did believed that justice should be done: a life for a life. That was the way it should be. However, Albert had always been a respecter of rules, so if the prison regulations said that Miss Florence Morton could come and visit, well so be it.

All the same, regulations notwithstanding, there was a whiff of something not quite right about the whole business. As a man who valued order and liked to see things done the proper way, Albert had initially been annoyed at the idea of this bold young woman, flaunting convention and pushing her way into what he thought of as *his* jail, but now that he was actually confronted with her, he saw that she was little more than a girl, screwing up her courage to accomplish what she evidently considered to be an important errand, and though he could not see what she hoped to gain by it, he couldn't but admire her nerve.

When they finally reached the room where the visit was to take place and he had pulled out the chair for her to sit down – not a courtesy he had ever extended to Brown's mother and sisters when they arrived, but somehow it had been automatic with Miss Morton – he reminded her that she must not attempt to push anything through the wire grill, nor take anything from Brown, if he attempted to make such a transaction the opposite way. After that Albert retired to a chair set in the furthest corner of the room, and observed the young woman – no more than twenty four or twenty five, at a guess – while she awaited the arrival of the prisoner, watching as she extracted a dainty, lace embroidered handkerchief from her bag and wiped her nose, then refolded the delicate little square and replaced it in her bag. After that she sat watching the door which led to the cell area, waiting for it to open.

Brown arrived a moment or two later, accompanied by Bottomley and Jordan, a couple of the warders who took turns to sit with him in pairs, on eight hourly shifts. Always two men in the cell with him and another on turnkey duty outside the door. You could take no chances with condemned men, though for the most part, they didn't make much trouble. There was always a bit of curiosity about the ones who'd been sent down for murder. How did he occupy himself, other officers had wanted to know? Residence in the condemned cell excused a man from work. He got better food and kinder companionship than the regular prisoners. Cards and dominoes were provided for his use. Brown was a keen card player, so they said. He received frequent visits from the chaplain, who had been encouraging him to read his bible. In between times he wrote letters to his folks in Huddersfield. And he remained optimistic about his release.

'Do you think he's guilty?' Albert had asked Joe Fazackerley, another of the men who had been detailed to sit with Brown.

'Well *he* doesn't think he is,' had been Joe's oblique reply.

'How do you fancy his chances with the appeal?' Albert had asked another of his fellow warders.

'I wouldn't put my shirt on him getting off.'

Possibly Brown was unaware of the generally held assessment. Certainly he did not look like a beaten man as he entered the room with a confident stride and his head held high. He was a taller than average man, with thick black hair and dark eyes which met another man's without flinching. He had the fresh complexion of someone accustomed to being out of doors, and though he was not obviously handsome, women undeniably found him attractive – which was where part of the trouble lay, if what Albert had read in the *Yorkshire Evening Post* was to be believed. There was nothing whatever in his appearance which endeared him to Albert, who saw him only as typical of a type: not bad looking, but a rough, working man, none the less, and one with a penchant for drinking and womanising, who had eventually been brought low by it.

'Miss Morton.' The prisoner inclined his head as he spoke, then sat down without waiting for an invitation.

'Mr Brown.'

Albert Henshaw took an audible breath of disapproval. There was no call for a lady like her to be addressing a man like that as 'Mr'.

There was a pause while each regarded the other, unsmiling, wondering.

'I trust they are feeding you well?'

It was what they all asked, Albert thought. Or variations on the theme. Are you being taken care of, given enough to eat, kept warm on these cold winter nights? Anyone would have thought it was a blasted hotel.

'Yes, thank you.'

There was silence again. If Brown knew what she had come for, he was giving her no help in getting to the point.

Eventually she said, 'Mr Brown… I have come to ask you… about the death of my brother.'

'I'm not sure as there's much I can tell you. I told everything I know in court. I'm very sorry for your loss,' he added, as if by way of an afterthought. 'I was fond of Fred. I'd known him since he were a lad.'

'I wasn't in court. My father thought it…unseemly.'

'But your father will have told you all that passed? And I expect you've read the papers.'

'I have.'

'I'm not allowed them in here. Well not the pages with the stuff about the trial. They let me see the sports pages. But my family have told me that pretty well all the evidence appeared in full.'

'So I believe,' she said. 'But some things about Fred's death remain unexplained. I believe there is more to be said.'

'Not by me.'

There was a pause before she spoke again. 'By someone else then? By Dorothy perhaps? Is that what you mean?'

'I meant nothing, except that I've already said everything that I can.'

'Mr Brown,' her voice, previously calm and level, took on a note of increasing urgency. 'Surely you must realise what peril you stand in. You are right when you say that I've read about the case. I've followed every word of it – and I feel sure that there is something more you are keeping back… And yes, I believe it concerns my sister-in-law, Dorothy.'

'There's to be an appeal. I don't expect to hang.'

The final word seemed to echo around the room, rebounding from the solid, painted brickwork, twisting itself around the bars at the window, until it splintered into fragments against the dirty window panes.

'So you continue to insist on your innocence, but refuse to say anything more?'

There was another pause. Brown seemed to be thinking. Eventually he said: 'Are you a Christian, Miss Morton?'

In his corner, Albert Henshaw bristled at the impropriety of such a question.

'I sincerely hope so, Mr Brown.'

'I've done some bad things in my time. Often in drink. There's been women and gambling and I even thieved some stuff when I were a lad, for which I was caught and punished, and quite right too. My poor Ma has shed a few tears over me, I'll tell you. I sometimes made my wife unhappy too, when she was alive – I could have been a kinder, better husband to her. But as God is my witness, I never shot a man in cold blood, Miss Morton. I never killed your brother.'

They sat in silence for a while, and again it was the young woman who broke it. She had been studying her gloved hands, clasped before her on the table, but she looked up at him as she said, 'And Dorothy's child, little Diana. Is there any chance that you, rather than Freddie, are the little girl's father?'

CHAPTER TWO

Monday 11 December 1933
Leeds Town Hall, The Yorkshire Assizes

His father had always told him, 'In any circus, son, it's as well to find out from the off, who the ring master is.'

Well on this, the first day of the trial, that was pretty obvious. From his position in the dock, Ernest Brown was looking straight across at the judge, with his slightly beaky nose and dimpled chin, his hair hidden under his ridiculous wig. The barristers too, were all done up like dog's dinners. Even the lesser minions, the ushers and note-takers wore flapping black gowns as they went about their business. All this bloody charade and play acting. He had no time for it, himself, but everyone kept on telling him that showmanship or not, you could trust the outcome. British justice was the finest in the world. If you're an innocent man, you have nothing to fear.

The court room was smaller than he had expected. Plainer. From his seat in the dock he looked down on the tables where the barristers sat, the little booth where the witnesses would give their evidence, and the benches for the jury. The public gallery was more elevated even than the judge's platform and lay directly behind the dock, so that he had to turn in his seat, in order to see who was there. He had only looked back there once, long enough to spot Ma, flanked by good old Doris, who was the best kind of daughter that his mother could ever have had. Charlie and Peggy were there too, but his father had stayed at home, his deafness precluding him from following the proceedings – and anyway someone had to be at home, when little Ethel came in from school. Poor old Ma, her face a study of worry. This should not have happened to Ma, who had enough on her plate already, what with making ends meet now that Dad could get no work, and matters gone from bad to worse with the money he had been sending to help keep Ethel, stopped ever since his arrest back in September. Ma said they had not told Ethel that her Daddy was in prison – the child merely thought him working away, as usual – but Ethel was seven years old and smart as paint, and who knew what she might have picked up in the school yard or overheard in the street?

Ernest had correctly anticipated that his own small group of relatives and supporters would be vastly outnumbered by the families from the other side. Dolly Morton's gang were there in force: her brother and her twin sister, both accompanied by their respective spouses, all of them wearing black, as a sign of their respect for Fred, he supposed, though none of them had had much time for him in life, if truth be told; and sitting a little apart from them, there was Fred's father, accompanied by his brother-in-law, Major McConnell, both of them men that Ernest knew well from the old days, when he had regularly paraded the shire horses belonging to his various employers around the rings at country shows. Frederick Morton Snr. did not look across at the man accused of murdering his son. Instead he gazed, unfocussed, into the middle distance, giving the impression of a man who had already taken too many nips at his hip flask, for all that it was so early in the day.

Not that he needs to look, Ernest thought, for he knows well enough who I am. He couldn't even remember how far back their acquaintance went, but he placed their first encounter to a time when he had been no more than a youngster of fifteen or so, working then for the old London and North Western Railway. Old Fred Morton had come up to compliment him on the turnout of a prize winning horse. It had been a kindly gesture, particularly since he had beaten Morton and Son's own horse and groom into second place. He fancied that young Fred had been with his father on that occasion, and him nobbut a lad of ten or eleven at the time, probably home from school for the holidays. He had won many a rosette for the London and North Western's stable. They had spotted the way he had with horses, when he was straight out of school. The beasts trusted him. He could sometimes be cruel to a human being, but never to an animal.

For some reason a vision of Mary slipped into his mind. He had not always been kind enough to Mary. Probably they should never have married – her still grieving for the husband she'd lost in the war, and him still hankering for the single life. He had been too young and she had been too sad, but there had been a baby on the way, so he had done the right thing. One bairn after another, but none of them had lived very long, saving for little Ethel, and though she had done her married duty, he often suspected that once she had Ethel, Mary had not really wanted him anymore, and so he had looked for companionship elsewhere, particularly after he went to work for young Fred Morton and began to live-in during the summer months, only going home occasionally – more to see Ethel than Mary – and once young Fred inherited the farm at Saxton Grange, the distance had been greater and his trips back to Huddersfield had become rarer still. Mary had taken badly in the winter of 1932 and died at Christmastime. It had been a shock, but these things happened, and as a working man could not take care of a child on his own, Ethel had gone to live with his mother, and his own life had gone on much as before.

There though… no sense dwelling on the past. What's done is done.

He was surprised to see that Dolly herself was not in the public gallery, but then he saw that she had been ushered into a place behind the table where the prosecution team was working. Her father, Harry Middlehurst, was sitting alongside her, glaring across at the dock, as if he would like to strangle Ernest with his bare hands. Dolly on the other hand was not looking his way at all. She was sitting upright and still, paying close attention to the proceedings, behaving in fact, as if she did not know that he was there at all. It was her ladylike, interested face, he thought. The one she would use in church and when dull company arrived, asking her to support a charitable concern, or inviting her to join in with some proposed social activity, against which she would ultimately make some excuse for non-attendance. He knew that face. He had seen her employing it plenty of times before.

He pulled his attention abruptly back to the present, for his moment was at hand. He took his cue and rose to his feet.

'Ernest Brown, you stand accused of the murder of Frederick Ellison Morton. How do you plead?'

He straightened his back and squared his shoulders. He might have deserted from the army, but he had not forgotten the way they taught a man how to stand. His words emerged with confidence and conviction: 'Not guilty, your lordship.'

Once he had resumed his seat between the two warders, it was the prosecuting barrister, Mr Paley Scott's turn in the spotlight. Ernest listened intently as he addressed the jury on behalf of the Crown. He had a way of speaking to them, Ernest noticed, which made it seem as if he had forgotten all about the people seated in the public gallery, the other gowns and wigs at the tables behind him, the scribbling shorthand writer, the man in the dock and even the judge himself: it was as if he was talking just to them, the most important people in the room.

His own counsel, Mr Streatfield, had warned him not to stare at the jury. 'Don't do anything at all which might make them feel as if you are sizing them up. Juries don't like that. They feel intimidated. You don't want them to think that you are in any way a dangerous man.'

So Ernest had barely glanced at the twelve men who would decide his fate. 'You have to trust them to make the right decision,' his solicitor, Mr Hyams, had said. 'Twelve good men and true. And Yorkshiremen too.' Ernest had once read that a man was entitled to be tried by a jury of his peers – which meant his equals – but of course he knew that was never going to happen, because jurymen were drawn from the list of local ratepayers, and ordinary working men, who lived in a tied cottage, or a rented tenement, or who lodged at the premises of their employers, as he had done until recently, would never appear on such a list.

Mr Paley Scott was a yarn spinner all right. He reminded Ernest of a man he had once known who frequented the Dog and Gun in Huddersfield. That chap had been a local man, so of course he hadn't actually sounded like Mr Paley Scott, but like the barrister, he could certainly tell the tale, always promising people that this or that horse was a sure thing. And not only horses. Candidates in the local elections, forthcoming football fixtures, why to listen to this chap you would think that he had the inside track on anything you should care to mention. It was never just his opinion, you understand. He'd always got the information from such and such a body, which proved without a shadow of a doubt that what he was about to tell you was correct. Ernest had been inclined to turn his back on the man in the pub at the first opportunity – Old Rattlebox, as he'd thought of him – but he paid the closest possible attention to every word from Mr Paley Scott. One of the problems they had faced all along, according to Mr Hyams, was not knowing precisely what the prosecution was going to say. Well now they would find out.

Mr Paley Scott began by telling the jury that 'the trouble' had begun when he, Ernest, had first been employed by Mr Frederick Morton Jnr., back in the summer of 1929. Of course, he did not say Ernest, or Ernie, or even Mr Brown. Just Brown, plain and simple, as befitted a man employed by Mr Morton, as a groom. Mr and Mrs Morton had kept quite a number of horses, Mr Paley Scott told the jury, and Brown had been responsible for looking after them, because Mr Morton had been very much occupied with running his substantial cattle factoring business (an enterprise concerned with the selling and leasing of cattle to the farming community, the prosecuting counsel explained, for the benefit of a jury largely drawn from townsfolk). In addition to taking care of the horses, Brown's duties had also included riding out with Mrs Dorothy Morton, in order to exercise the hunters. After this arrangement had been ongoing for some time, 'a state of physical intimacy' had developed between them, Mr Paley Scott said, to which Mrs Morton had initially been a willing party.

Out of the corner of his eye, Ernest could see the journalists, on their benches, scribbling frantically. Groom and mistress had an affair. That was the kind of headline which would sell an extra paper or two, though it might not be put in precisely those terms, because public delicacy must not be offended, for all that most of the public would secretly want to know all about it. So not those exact words perhaps. He himself had never been much of a man for words. He had never wanted to be.

'The affair went on for almost a year,' Mr Paley Scott continued, his tone carefully neutral, 'but Mrs Morton finally decided that it must stop.'

'Whatever is said, try not to show any emotion,' Mr Hyams had advised him. 'Even if you completely disagree, or feel that something has been said which is unfair or untrue.'

'The man Brown refused to accept that their affair was over. He threatened Mrs Morton that if she discontinued their relationship, he would tell her husband. Imagine this poor woman's dilemma. Mrs Morton now found herself completely at the mercy of this man, who had it in his power to destroy her marriage and ruin her good name. When she attempted to resist his advances, the man Brown offered her violence, sometimes punching and kicking her. Mrs Morton dared not let her husband see the results of these attacks upon her person. Instead she continued to conceal the truth from her husband, Frederick Morton, and continued to submit to those acts which she now found so odious.

'Mrs Morton will appear before you, gentlemen of the jury and testify about this terrible ordeal. She will tell you how, as time went on, she became increasingly afraid of the man Brown, but of course, she still dared not tell her husband and so Brown grew ever more confident of his hold over her. Then in June, earlier this year, Brown abruptly left the Morton household, following an argument about his duties. Mrs Morton was of course, greatly relieved by Brown's departure, but alas this respite from his unwelcome attentions was short-lived, because within a matter of three days Brown had returned, demanding that she get him reinstated and threatening her with violence, should she fail to do so. His position as groom had already been filled, so the best Mrs Morton could do was to persuade her husband to take Brown on as a general handyman – a role which was not so much to his liking as his previous work had been. The Crown will bring witnesses who will testify to Brown's increasing animosity and resentment towards Mr Frederick Morton from that time onward; and in the meantime of course, the unfortunate Mrs Morton was reluctantly forced to resume her previous relationship with Brown.'

Mr Paley Scott paused theatrically allowing the full import of his words to settle in the minds of the observers in the public gallery, on the journalists (who were already deciding which euphemisms they would be forced to employ, in order to titillate, without offending, their loyal readers) and most of all upon the jury. Ernest resisted the temptation to glance over his shoulder at the public gallery, but he could imagine the way the various members of the Morton and Middlehurst families were all staring straight ahead, doing their best to retain composure, in the face of poor Dolly's disgrace. A few indiscretions with your own kind was one thing, but being caught out with a man of the servant class was quite another.

Instead Ernest fixed his eyes on the coat of arms above the judge's head, the golden lion and unicorn standing out as if their gilding had been freshly applied. In spite of trying to apply his full concentration elsewhere, Ernest was aware that some of the jurors were weighing him up, considering his good physique, his obvious strength, the large, work hardened hands, which could be employed to calm a horse, caress a mistress, or slap a woman around, as their owner chose.

Having allowed a moment or two for his words to sink in, Mr Paley Scott resumed. 'The Crown will show that on Tuesday 5 September this year, Brown's disenchantment with his position and his continuing obsession with Mrs Morton combined to fatal effect. That evening, having threatened and assaulted Mrs Morton, he lay in wait for Mr Morton to return home, terrorising Mrs Morton and her resident companion, Miss Ann Houseman, and cutting the telephone wires to prevent them from summoning help. When Mr Morton returned home that night, Brown shot him dead at close range, and later attempted to conceal this dreadful crime, by placing Mr Morton's body in his car, then setting alight the garage in which it stood.

'This fire was initially represented as a terrible accident, with Brown himself playing the role of hero – rescuing his late employer's animals and alerting the local fire brigade – but gentlemen of the jury, fate can sometimes play a hand in the annals of justice. Though that fire was fuelled by petrol, and a whole variety of other combustibles, though the heat from it was so terrible, that the building itself, and the two motor cars within it were completely destroyed, together with almost every remnant of the unfortunate Frederick Morton's body, a very small part of the victim's torso had survived the blaze. The physician called upon to examine this charred fragment, the last mortal remains of Mr Frederick Morton, was Dr Sutherland, and he will appear before you and testify to finding a piece of wadding and a number of shotgun pellets, lodged near the victim's heart. It seems little short of Divine Providence, that this one surviving section of the body, should be the part which would betray the truth of Mr Frederick Morton's fate.

'The Crown will demonstrate not only that Mr Morton died at another man's hand, but also that the guilty party was the man who stands charged before you, Ernest Brown.'

Divine Providence, Mr Paley Scott had called it. Ernest considered the phrase, while the final echoes of the prosecuting barrister's oration rang around the court. He had not heard it called that before. He distinctly recalled that someone in the press had written a piece which said that from the point of view of the murderer, the fluky survival of that particular part of the body was a stroke of bad luck.

Though he was careful not to turn and stare, Ernest had been able to glance over his shoulder a couple more times during the opening speeches, and noted that once the various close family members had been accommodated, the remaining seats in the gallery had been occupied by other members of the public: older women mostly (younger women would be at home, minding their children, and men of course, had to be at work). He was astonished to see that some of these old women had even come equipped with knitting, or were covertly fishing into paper bags for boiled sweets. The warders who accompanied him to court had told him that some of them would have been queuing up outside for hours, in order to get a place. Ernest had never thought of a courtroom as a place of entertainment before.

During this first morning, the old biddies, as Ernest thought of them, had given their fullest attention to the commencement of the proceedings, and particularly to the swearing in of the jury and the all-important moment when he had been confronted with the charge and had registered his firm 'Not guilty.' There had been a palpable frisson of excitement in the room, when Mr Paley Scott had spoken of an affair between himself and Dorothy Morton, and he could almost feel the disapproving stares in his direction, when the prosecution counsel had talked of the violence he was accused of inflicting upon Dolly. Ernest, though well aware of the waves of hostility which were sweeping across the room towards him, had continued to listen intently to Mr Paley Scott, showing no emotion.

No doubt the old biddies were all eagerly anticipating some more salacious revelations, because there was a distinct sense of anti-climax in the gallery, when the first prosecution witness turned out to be a draftsman, who had produced plans of the farm and the outbuildings which surrounded it, for the use of the court. The judge spent an age poring over the drawings, asking all manner of daft questions about the position of doors and windows, and grilling the fellow in the witness box as though he himself were the one on trial.

'There are some gates shown here, are they in the right place?'

'Yes, my lord.'

'Do you know which way they open?'

'They open outwards.'

'Is that indicated on the plan?'

'Yes, my lord.'

Ernest could see that the draughtsman was being patient and respectful, though he must have been thinking that the old fool could surely see for himself what had been plainly drawn on the plans. He sympathised with the fellow in the witness box. The likes of us are forever having to keep our voices polite and our faces straight, he thought, while silly old buggers who think themselves our betters, ask damn fool questions.

When His Honour Travers Humphreys had finished deliberating over the farm house, the garages, the stables, sheds and barns, he turned his attention to the part of the drawing which showed the small hut to the east of the house and the main yard, where Ernest himself had slept. How many windows were there? Did they open? Were the windows particularly dirty?

'They were neither particularly dirty, nor particularly clean, my lord.'

Daft old sod. What on earth had the windows in his hut got to do with the price of fish, Ernest wondered?

When the plans had finally been accepted into the evidence, it was the turn of the police photographer to take the stand. He had provided an album of pictures taken both at the scene and at the mortuary, which also had to be sworn into evidence. There was a flutter of interest among the old biddies when Mr Paley Scott, full of affected concern, commented that 'Some of the photographs are of a distressing nature, my lord, and it may be possible to spare the jury from seeing them.'

The judge spent a long time peering at the pictures himself, while everyone else covertly and vainly craned their necks in an unsuccessful bid to see what he was looking at, and eventually, after a brief discussion between himself and the senior barristers appearing for either side, the judge announced that it had been agreed to withhold the photographs which had been numbered nine and ten from the jury. From his position in the dock, Ernest fancied that he could sense disappointment from the old biddies. (Not that they would ever have been close enough to see the photographs for themselves, even if they had been put forward in the evidence.) They were the sort of women who would tut at his own conduct, Ernest thought, but were not ashamed to sit in a public court room, in the hopes of wallowing in every sordid detail of another woman's affair and another man's death. He spared them the briefest of glances again, while he pretended to be flexing his neck. All got up in their best hats and coats, as if for an outing. You wouldn't have caught his own Ma attending this sort of carry-on unless she had to.

He guessed that it was the appearances of himself and Dolly Morton in the witness box, that the old biddies had really come for, but they still had a while to wait for that. First there was a procession of policemen, swearing that the various bits and pieces brought from Saxton Grange were one and the same with the things that were now being produced in court. Ernest had once been to see a music hall act, where a fellow got up in a red lined cloak and a silk top hat had produced a lot of unlikely looking stuff, one item after another, from out of a little box which looked far too small to have contained any of it, and he thought that this motley collection of objects, each of them placed in turn on a table midway between the judge's platform and the enclosure where he sat himself, each of them labelled with a letter, so that they could be called 'Exhibit A' and 'Exhibit B', reminded him of the fellow's act in a funny sort of way, except that here everyone sat rapt in silence, whereas at the music hall there had been raucous shouts: 'Yon sword's made of rubber' and 'There's an hole in the bottom of your box, mate!'

It was a funny collection of stuff, when you got right down to it. The photograph album, all new and pristine, a couple of kitchen knives, a length of old rope, a shotgun and a box of cartridges, a pair of badly burned pliers, found amid the wreckage of the fire, which had supposedly been used to loosen the plates on the bottom of the cars' petrol tanks. A neat little pile of his own folded clothes and perhaps most incongruous of all, a pair of work boots, standing neatly at the end of the line. A right old jumble sale gone wrong, in fact.

Even when that lot had all been got through, it still wasn't Dorothy Morton's turn, for first they had to hear from PC Broadhead, who had been on the premises when the fire was finally put out and the wreckage examined for any signs that Frederick Morton had been inside the garage when it burned down. Though Broadhead did his best to explain the way that roof slates and wooden beams had fallen down onto the two cars, Ernest doubted that even the official photographs fully conveyed the scene of devastation which had confronted everyone that morning, after the fire brigade had finished damping down. Once it was cool enough to approach what remained of the barn, the village constable explained, it had not taken him long to confirm the fears of the waiting family members and farm workers alike. Lying across the buckled springs of what had once been the front seats of the Chrysler motor car, he had uncovered all that remained of the master of Saxton Grange. A good part of his body, all his clothing and facial features had been destroyed, but among the debris close by, Broadhead had found a set of keys and a man's dress ring, both badly burned, but still easily identifiable as belonging to Fred Morton.

'You say that when you found what remained of the torso, it appeared as if Mr Morton had been lying across the seats?'

'Yes sir.'

By the time both barristers had finished drawing out the evidence of Constable Broadhead, the day was over. They had spent so much time on the preliminaries, Ernest thought, what with the speeches and drawings and photographs and such like, they had barely got on to the meat of the matter at all. Even after the weeks spent on remand, he had yet to become accustomed to sitting still for so long. His had been a life of fresh air and physical activity, and winter or not, he longed to return to it. Once this blooming trial was over, he wanted nothing more than to saddle up a horse and ride out in the open air. He imagined the sound of the hooves, beating on the turf, the horse's breathing, his own heart beating in tune with it all, but instead came the sharp command that all should rise, as His Lordship Travers Humphreys quit the room.

CHAPTER THREE

Tuesday 12 December 1933
Leeds Town Hall, The Yorkshire Assizes

There was a perceptible stir in the public gallery as the usher called on Mrs Dorothy Morton to take the witness stand. As she rose from her position beside her father and crossed the narrow strip of floor to gain the witness box, she had to pass close in front of the dock, but she did not so much as glance at the man who sat there, though he never took his eyes off her. A tall, slim figure in the dark, well cut suit, which marked her widow hood. A little fur draped around her shoulders and an expensive hat, on which the papers were sure to comment. A delicately powdered face, handsome rather than pretty, with fashionably reddened lips, the colour of over-ripe strawberries. The court had fallen so silent that the delicate tap of her neat little heels was clearly audible to those seated in the public gallery.

Mr Paley Scott led his principal witness gently into her evidence, inviting Dolly to say how long she and Freddie Morton had been married, where they had initially made their home, how long it was since he had inherited Saxton Grange from an uncle, and how they had only begun to live there on a permanent basis in January of the previous year. When Paley Scott's questions moved on to the man in the dock himself, she agreed that Ernest Brown had worked for her husband for about four years, although the two men had known one another for much longer, having had regular contact at livestock shows and markets for a number of years, before her husband had offered Brown employment as a groom: 'We needed a groom because we kept a lot of horses: both for our own use and because I ran a small riding school.'

'And Brown's duties included riding out with you, to help exercise the horses?'

'That is correct.'

'He is a fine horseman, is he not?'

'Yes.'

Ernest kept his eyes fixed upon her, but Dolly still did not look his way.

'And during these expeditions together, an association grew up between you?'

'Yes.'

'Intimacy took place?'

'Yes.' She continued to look straight at Mr Paley Scott. No flinching, no embarrassment. She might have been answering questions about her grocery order.

'You were initially a willing participant?'

'Initially, yes.'

'How long did this state of affairs persist?'

'For about twelve months. After that I wanted to end it and I tried to turn away his advances.'

'And how did Brown take this rejection?'

'He did not like it. He became threatening.'

'In what way?'

'He said that he would tell my husband.'

'Did he offer you violence?'

'Yes.'

From the dock, Ernest willed her to look at him, but Dolly continued to focus her full attention on Mr Paley Scott.

'So you had to go on accepting this man's advances – even though you did not want to?'

'Yes.'

'You did not tell your husband.'

'I was afraid to.'

'So matters between yourself and the accused continued as before.'

'Yes.'

'Was Brown a jealous man?'

'Very jealous.'

'Can you tell the court in what way this jealousy manifested itself?'

'Well… For example on one occasion, Brown saw me talking to another man and he threatened to strangle me.'

'To strangle you?' Paley Scott repeated it slowly and clearly, allowing everyone to dwell as long as possible over the words.

'Yes.'

'Your husband was frequently away from home on business?'

'Yes.'

'When your husband was away, was there anyone else to whom you could look for protection?'

'No one. Not until the arrival of Miss Houseman, who was employed from the end of July this year, as my companion and to help look after the baby.'

'Apart from your husband and your child, Mrs Morton, how many people normally spent the night at your farm?'

'Only Brown and Miss Houseman slept on the premises.'

'Miss Houseman inside the house and Brown in a hut nearby?'

'That is correct.'

'Did something happen in June last year, which altered the situation in respect of Brown?'

'Yes. Brown left his job at Saxton Grange in June and went back to his people in Huddersfield.'

'He left of his own accord?'

'Yes. He had been asked to cut the lawn. He said that wasn't part of his duties, lost his temper and walked out.'

'Your husband immediately replaced him.'

'Yes, we could not be without a groom.'

'But then Brown wanted his job back?'

'Yes. He walked out on the Tuesday, but then he telephoned me later the same day, asking for his job back and when I declined to take him back on, the next day he wrote me a letter, asking the same thing.'

'What did you do with the letter?'

'I destroyed it. I destroy all my correspondence.'

'Did you write back to him?'

'Yes. I told him that his position had been filled.'

'What happened then?'

'On the Friday of that week he turned up at the farm. I was alone in the house. He came inside and demanded that I get him reinstated.'

'Did Brown threaten you on this occasion?'

'He did.'

'In what way?'

'He said that he would strangle me, if I did not get him his job back.'

'Where was your husband at this time?'

'He was at Carlisle. He went there every Friday for the cattle market.'

'So Brown would have known that he would be away from home that day?'

'Yes.'

'What did you do in the face of these threats?'

'I telephoned my husband, at the hotel where I knew that he ate his lunch in Carlisle. I told him that Brown had turned up, asking for his old position, but of course, Freddie said that the role had already been filled. I relayed this to Brown and he made a gesture with his hands – like someone wringing a chicken's neck – so I asked Freddie – I pleaded with him, really – whether there wasn't some other job available on the farm that Brown could have, and Freddie said that we could take him back on as a kind of handyman.'

'So from June last year, your husband re-employed Brown as a handyman. Was he happy with that situation?'

'No. He did not like the new job. He became ever more unkind and disrespectful.'

Ernest watched for the slightest sign of hesitation, but there was none. Dolly would make an excellent impression, he thought, with her confident delivery, and that clear articulation which reached the furthest corners of the court room. She held her head as erect as if she were on horseback, showing off her handsome features to their best advantage. He found himself picturing her in the paddock back at Saxton Grange, bareheaded, in her jodhpurs and blouse, instructing some kiddie on a pony at the end of a leading rein. In his mind's eye, he saw her glance across at him, as he passed the paddock gate, her momentary expression full of invitations and promises.

Ernest sensed a lessening of interest among the old biddies, while Mr Paley Scott, having safely re-established Ernest in his new role at the farm, began to question Dolly on a variety of other matters, including the various motor vehicles which were kept at Saxton Grange. There was the Chrysler which her husband had habitually driven, the Essex, which was a general runabout, used by both the women in the household, and the horsebox, which was used whenever the need arose to transport livestock by road. On the evening of Tuesday 5 September, she explained, her husband had been out on business in the Chrysler, Brown had been out making a delivery with the horsebox and Miss Houseman had been out on an errand in the Essex, which on her return she had parked at the top of the drive, where it would normally be left for Brown to put it into the garage later (the unspoken fact of the matter, Ernest thought, being that this was a manoeuvre quite beyond the limited driving skills of young Ann Houseman).

Any heads which had been nodding soon went up again, when Mr Paley Scott asked his witness to tell him what had happened that day in more detail. Finally, they were getting to the nitty gritty of the matter. Dolly began slowly and carefully, not Ernest thought, as if there was any doubt about what she had to say, but rather as if she were determined to leave nothing out.

'My husband left the house at about one thirty that afternoon. He had some business to attend to in Oldham. It's about an hour's run from Saxton Grange in each direction, and he said that he would be back at about six o'clock. We usually ate our meal at about six thirty. Brown had been sent out in the horsebox at around noon, and he was also expected back in the early evening.'

'Would the entire household usually have sat down to a meal together?' enquired Mr Paley Scott.

'Oh no. My husband, myself and Miss Houseman ate together in the dining room and Brown would have his supper at the kitchen table. As my husband had not returned at six thirty, Miss Houseman and I ate ours – it was a cold supper that night – and my husband's meal was left out in the dining room.'

'And Brown's supper?'

'That was always left on the kitchen table, ready for him to eat whenever he had finished his chores.'

'So both men's suppers had been left out, pending their return. Pray continue, Mrs Morton.'

'There had been a good lot of fruit picked in the preceding days and the maids had prepared it that afternoon, ready for us to make some jam when the temperature dropped a little, but after the maids had all gone home, I realised that we hadn't got a jam pan, so I sent Ann off in the Essex car to borrow one from some of our neighbours. When she got back we sat in the garden for a while and then we went inside and Baby was fed and put to bed, and Ann started on the jam, while I did other small jobs about the farm and the house.'

'Thank you. Kindly tell the court what happened next.'

'Brown returned at about eight thirty. He drove the horse box straight down the drive and into the yard, where I was filling water buckets at the trough. He got down from the cab and asked me if the boss was in – that was what all the men called my husband. I said that he wasn't. Brown then asked me where I had been that afternoon and I told him that I had been bathing, in the river at Wetherby.'

Mr Paley Scott interposed with yet another of his useful little prompts. 'I do not ask you for the name, but did you tell him that you had been bathing with a man?'

No names, no pack drill, Ernest thought, with an inward smile. No one's husband is going to have any explaining to do.

'Yes.'

'You told him the man's name, and it was a name which would have been known to him?'

'Yes.'

Me and half the ruddy county, Ernest thought.

'What happened then?'

'Brown flew into a rage. He got hold of me and pushed me into the mistal, then he banged my head against the wall and threw me on the floor. I was very much afraid of him and what he might do. I managed to get out into the yard, but he grabbed me again and tried to push me into the horsebox, and in desperation, I shouted for Ann. Then he grabbed me and pushed me into the barn. He had me pressed up against the wall and he had his hands on my throat, but at that moment we both heard Ann coming across the yard, so he pushed me away and put his finger to his lips.

'Ann came then and asked me if I'd called. I said "no" and then I walked back to the house with her. She went into the kitchen, but I went straight up to the nursery. I had only been there a couple of minutes, when Ann came upstairs and said that Brown was in the kitchen, wanting to talk to me, but I told her that I couldn't come down just then, and she went back downstairs.'

'Why did you not go downstairs just then?'

'I was trying to avoid Brown.'

'And what happened next, Mrs Morton?'

'After a few minutes, I went down to the kitchen and found that Brown was still in there, with Ann, so I asked him what he wanted to speak with me about and he told me about a cow he had fetched back in the horsebox and then he went outside. A few minutes later, he came back in again and asked me if I would go outside to help him put the ducks away for the night, but I said that I couldn't as I was expecting a phone call from my father.'

'Was that the real reason?' Mr Paley Scott interposed, smooth and helpful as ever.

'No. I told him that because I did not wish to go outside as I was frightened of him. He went out alone and I took up my sewing, while Ann carried on making the jam.'

'And what was the next out of the ordinary thing to occur?'

'We heard a shot.'

'Were any guns kept at the farm?'

'Only one. A shotgun which belonged to my husband. It was normally kept in the kitchen cupboard.'

'You have no gun of your own?'

'No, not at present. I had a shotgun at one time, but I have it no longer.'

'So you heard a shot. Can you tell us any more about this shot and about what you did next?'

'It sounded as if some pellets had hit the kitchen window. Until then I had not realised that anyone had taken the gun out of the cupboard. It was about half past nine by then and getting dark. Miss Houseman and I both jumped and ran out of the kitchen, and along the hall, to the front door.'

'Why did you run towards the front door, when the shots had come from the other side of the house?'

'We were frightened. We ran to the front door, to get away from Brown. I went and hid in the dining room, under the table, while Miss Houseman went back to the kitchen, but a few minutes later when I heard her talking to Brown in the kitchen, I went back in there too.'

'Did you ask Brown what he had been doing with the gun?'

'No. But Ann... Miss Houseman, asked him.'

'She will tell us about that, in her evidence. What happened next?'

'At about nine forty the telephone rang. Brown was not in the kitchen just then. Miss Houseman and I both went into the drawing room to answer it, and as we entered the drawing room, we saw Brown coming downstairs. Until then, neither of us had realised that he had gone upstairs.'

'Should he have been upstairs?'

'No. He had no right to be up there.'

'Very well. Please continue. The telephone was ringing.'

'Ann answered the telephone and it was someone wanting to speak with my husband. He was already well overdue, so Ann suggested that they should call back shortly – say in about fifteen minutes.

'After that we went back to the kitchen and a few minutes later Brown came in and took the game knife – that is the knife with a white handle – from the drawer in the dresser. He took it outside for a couple of minutes, then brought it back and put it in the drawer. We were both expecting the telephone to ring again any minute, but it never did. Then Brown bobbed back out again and came in with the shotgun. He laid it on the dresser and sat down next to it and asked Ann to leave the room, as he had something he wanted to say to me alone.'

'And what did Miss Houseman say to that?'

'Ann said she would not go out. She told him that if he had anything to say, he could say it in front of her. He said something like, "It would be much better for you, if you went out," but she still refused to go. Then he picked up the gun and sat looking at it. It was making us even more nervous, so Miss Houseman said to him, "Give me the gun."'

'And what was his reaction to that?'

'Brown took the gun apart and started cleaning it. Before he did that, he offered it to Miss Houseman, but she declined to take hold of it. His expression was dreadful.'

The judge leaned forward an inch or two in his chair. 'Can you explain to us what you mean by that?'

Dolly appeared momentarily thrown off course by the interruption. 'Well… we were very frightened of him…'

Everyone looked expectantly at Mr Justice Humphreys. Did that elaborate the matter sufficiently? But the judge looked down at his notes, then up at the court in general, giving no clue and after waiting a moment, Mr Paley Scott prompted the witness with another of his invitations to explain what had happened next.

'When he had finished cleaning the gun, he put it away, in its usual place in the cupboard. Then he went outside again. He must have gone to his hut, because when he came back in the next time, he was wearing his bedroom slippers. He brought the dog into the kitchen with him. Not our pet dog, but the guard dog, Zara, a great dane. Then, at around eleven thirty he went outside again and soon afterwards we heard the wheels of a car, coming past the kitchen.'

Mr Paley Scott jumped in again, asking Dolly a series of questions which served to remind her listeners that the drive which led into the property from the lane came straight past the kitchen, so that any vehicles which came down the drive to the garage, had to pass with a few feet of the kitchen door and would therefore be clearly audible to anyone inside.

'You heard only the wheels on the gravel, not the sound of the engine?'

'Just the wheels. We often freewheeled the cars down the drive, with the engines switched off.'

'And after you had heard the wheels of the car, what then?' the prosecuting counsel asked.

'Brown came back in again and I asked him if what we had heard had been my husband coming in. He said it was, but that my husband had told him that he was going out again. After that we all three sat in the kitchen. Several times, Brown tried to persuade Miss Houseman to go up to bed, but she refused to retire for the night without me. Eventually, at about ten minutes to midnight, we both went up to our respective bedrooms, but I was too afraid of what Brown might do to go to sleep and instead of undressing, I locked myself in the bathroom, which overlooks the yard. After I had been there for about half an hour, I saw Brown, creeping about in the yard. Later on I saw him unlock the kitchen door with his key and then I heard him coming upstairs and creeping about on the landing. After a while, Ann came to me in the bathroom and then we went and sat in her room. From time to time we heard Brown creeping about in the house. We were absolutely terrified.'

Dolly paused, perhaps to catch her breath, perhaps to allow the import of her words to impress themselves upon the minds of the jurors. After a moment she continued: 'At around three or half past three in the morning, I heard a bang and a cracking sound and when I went to the window, I saw that the garage was on fire. We ran downstairs to telephone for the police, but the line was dead. Ann ran back up to the nursery for the baby, while I fetched some rugs to wrap ourselves in. After that we ran out of the front door and into the garden, where we hid, under the front hedge. I could hear Brown shouting "Mrs Morton", but we didn't answer him.'

'And after you heard him calling out your name, what then?'

'We heard him shouting some more and running about and then we heard the horsebox starting up. At that point we set off for Towton, cutting across the fields the whole way. I could see the lights of the horsebox, as Brown drove it along the main road, towards the village. When Miss Houseman and I reached the village we went straight to Mr Stuart's house – he is our farm foreman – and from there another of the villagers who has a car drove me back to the farm.'

'And soon after you arrived back at the farm, did you and Mr Stuart search the house together?'

'We did.'

'And did you notice anything unusual in the house?'

'I noticed that my husband's supper was still on the dining table and that Brown's was still on the kitchen table and that both meals were untouched. We also found a coil of rope, lying on the floor of the landing, outside my bedroom door.' Dolly paused again in her recital. 'Also the drawing room window was wide open and there was a muddy mark, like a footprint, on the cushion of the window seat.'

'Had Brown also returned to the farm?'

'Yes. He was helping to fight the fire.'

'Did you have any conversation with him?'

'Yes. Initially I told him to play the hose on the loose box, in order to prevent the fire from spreading. Later, I asked him if he had had anything to do with the fire. He said he had not. Then he said, "If you tell anyone anything, I shall hang you with that rope on the landing."'

CHAPTER FOUR

Tuesday 12 December 1933
Leeds Town Hall, The Yorkshire Assizes

Mr Paley Scott signalled that he had finished his
questions by thanking the witness and politely inclining
his head. Good grief, Ernest thought, the man might
have been acknowledging that she had provided him
with a good luncheon or something.

It was his own counsel's turn now. Ernest leaned
forward in the dock and watched intently as Mr
Streatfield took his time, pausing to sip from his water
glass, dab his lips with a white napkin, then spend a
moment consulting his notes. Unlike Mr Paley Scott,
whose tone had been encouraging, almost friendly, when
Mr Streatfield eventually addressed Dorothy Morton, it
was in the chiding voice of a schoolmaster, attempting to

extract a confession from a recalcitrant pupil, when both parties know perfectly well that the scholar in question has been out of bounds.

'Now, Mrs Morton, you have told the court that you were originally a willing participant in this… friendship… with the accused man.'

'That is correct.' Dorothy held her head erect and met his eye.

From the rear of the gallery came a hiss which sounded suspiciously akin to 'brazen hussy'.

'But then something made you change your mind.' Mr Streatfield cut across the attempted interruption, before the judge even had time to censure the offender, or threaten to have them removed from the proceedings.

'Yes. I came to dislike him intensely.' Dorothy too, behaved as if she had not heard the lone expression of condemnation.

'I put it to you, Mrs Morton, that what changed your feelings for my client, was the discovery last summer, that he had been unfaithful to you?'

'No.'

'Isn't it the case that you had a number of conversations with Ernest Brown, in which you upbraided him for paying attentions to other women in the district?'

'No, it is not.' She spoke in the same quiet, firm voice that she had used throughout.

There must surely have been something to bring about this change of heart on your part.' Streatfield paused, but when no response was forthcoming, he put a further question: 'Can you tell the court exactly when it was that you suddenly decided that you did not like Ernest Brown after all?'

'Not the exact time. It was about three years ago.'

'Three years ago? And yet you continued to be intimate with him?'

'He forced me to.'

'For three years?'

'Yes.'

'And when did the last act of intimacy take place?'

'In June, last year.'

'So for almost *three years*,' Streatfield repeated the claim with renewed emphasis, 'this man – an employee – forced you to engage in these acts which you say you found so distasteful?'

'I was terrified of him.'

'Was there no means of avoiding his attentions? For example by say, locking yourself in the bathroom, as you have told the court that you did in the early hours of 6 September?'

'If I had locked the door against him, it would only have made him worse, in the long run.'

'And you say that your husband knew nothing of all this?'

'No. I was afraid to tell my husband.'

'Were you afraid of your husband too?'

'No. I was afraid of what Brown might do to me if I told my husband.'

'But surely, if you had told your husband, he would immediately have sent this man packing?'

'If my husband had sent him away, or complained to the police, I knew that Brown would eventually come back and harm me.'

'Isn't it true that Ernest Brown voluntarily left your husband's employment, in June last year? Why, when you thought him gone, did you not take advantage of his absence, to tell your husband all that he had done to you?'

'I knew that Brown would come back.'

'How could you be so sure?'

'He had threatened me many times.'

'Was that really the reason, Mrs Morton? Was it not the case that you wrote to him, asking him to return?'

'Of course not.'

'But when he came back – what, two, three days later – didn't you help him get his job back?'

'He left on the Tuesday and returned on the Friday. I did not want to take him back on, but he threatened to kill me, if I did not intercede with my husband and get him his job back.'

'You have told the court, I think, that Ernest Brown made some kind of gestures, while you were on the telephone. Can I ask you how he could have done that, when in his own recollection, he was standing in the doorway, holding your baby daughter at the time?'

'He was not holding the baby. She was upstairs, asleep in the nursery at the time.'

'I am sorry to say that I shall have to ask you some more questions of a personal nature, Mrs Morton.' Mr Streatfield's voice took on such a note of solemnity, that he might have been giving notice of a bereavement. 'You and your husband each rather went your own way, did you not?'

For the first time, Dorothy displayed the very slightest hesitation before answering. 'We were very happy together, most of the time.'

'But not all the time?'

'I think everyone has some difficult times.'

'Was your late husband fond of female society, Mrs Morton?'

'I really don't know what you mean.'

'Let me put it another way. I think I am right in saying that your husband often came home very late and on some occasions, he did not come home at all?'

'That was only on one occasion.'

'What was only on one occasion?'

Dorothy Morton's voice dropped momentarily. 'When he did not come home at all.'

'But he was often very late...' After a long pause, Streatfield added, 'Kindly answer the question, Mrs Morton.'

'I was not aware that it was a question. Yes, he was often away until late.'

'And you too had various other friends?'

'I am very fond of society.'

'I am sure that is so. I am referring, as I am sure you are aware, to male society. Let us again consider the man Ernest Brown and the relations which existed between you. When this intimacy first occurred between yourself and this particular man, did you give him any encouragement?'

'No.'

'What did you say?' asked the defence counsel, who along with the rest of the assembly had heard the answer perfectly clearly.

'No.'

'Now come, Mrs Morton. You were the mistress and he was the groom. You ask us to believe that simply by going out riding with you, he came to be on these extremely familiar terms with you, the wife of his employer, without receiving any encouragement whatsoever from you?'

'Yes.'

'So you ask us to believe that a groom can really get on intimate terms with his mistress, without any encouragement, and that this sad state of affairs can continue, for up to a year with your consent, but without your encouragement.'

'Yes.'

You had to admire her, Ernest thought. How many women could stand before a packed courtroom and answer questions such as these without betraying so much as a flush of embarrassment? There was none as could say that Dolly Morton lacked spirit, whether it be out on the hunting field, or facing up to a hawk faced fellow in an off-white wig.

'As a matter of fact, you and Brown continued to be on intimate terms up until June last year, did you not?'

'Not with my consent.'

'Are you really saying not only that Ernest Brown succeeded in initiating this relationship without any encouragement whatsoever from you, but also that for the best part of three years, you then submitted to his attentions only because he was threatening you? And that during all this time, your husband never noticed anything which he questioned in your manner, and that you, yourself, never complained to your husband? You never suggested to your husband that he should get rid of this man, who was making such a hell of your life? You never attempted to hash up some sort of accusation, or excuse to get him fired?'

Was it just a change in the light, or had the faintest flush appeared in Dolly's perfectly powdered cheeks?

'I should have been very pleased to get rid of him.'

'But you did nothing to bring it about?'

'I do not remember.'

'Were you aware that Brown was paying attention to any other women at any time?'

'No.'

'You are sure about that?'

'Absolutely.'

'Were you paying attentions to any other men?'

'No.'

'I am sorry, Mrs Morton, but I am afraid we shall have to go into this matter more deeply. Let me be more specific. Were you paying attentions to the man – we will not mention his name – with whom you told the court that you had bathed in the river, on the afternoon of Tuesday 5 September?'

'No.'

'This man is married, I think. Was the man's wife present when you met him to go swimming that afternoon?'

'No.'

'Was anyone else present?'

'No.'

'Last summer, were you and another man on the same sort of intimate terms that you had previously enjoyed with Brown?'

'No.'

Streatfield momentarily half turned to face the jury, his eyebrows raised, before returning his entire attention back to the woman in the witness box. 'But is it not the case that you were surprised in an embrace with a man, in the nursery at Saxton Grange, last summer?' he asked.

'Yes, that is true.'

'And this man with whom you were discovered in the nursery was not your husband, nor the groom, Ernest Brown, nor the man with whom you went bathing in the river.'

'No.

'This man with whom you were engaged in an embrace in the nursery was a different man, was it not? A man who had succeeded Ernest Brown in your affections, during the summer of this year?'

For a moment Dorothy Morton said nothing, but Mr Streatfield stood before her, waiting in expectant silence, compelling a reply. Eventually she said: 'I was intimate with this other man, yes.'

It was the first real concession she had made. The old biddies in the public gallery leant forward as a body, but if they had hoped for any further salacious revelations they were destined to be disappointed. The man who had enjoyed Dorothy Morton's favours last summer would not be named. Ernest spared a glance in the direction of Mr Justice Humphreys and immediately sensed his disapproval. Dolly Morton might have behaved like a common trollop, but she was a woman from a good local family and with all this talk of socialism and the like, Judge Humphreys and his kind would see no value in her public humiliation. Ernest experienced the strongest sensation that Mr Streatfield had just secured an almighty own goal.

Fixing Mr Streatfield with a particularly steely glare, Travers Humphreys interposed to announce that the court would adjourn for lunch.

CHAPTER FIVE

Tuesday 12 December 1933
Leeds Town Hall, The Yorkshire Assizes

Down in the cell below the court, Ernest sat with his usual pair of warders, chewing on a dry ham sandwich. Hopes of a good feed had been falsely raised when one of the warders had mentioned to him the day before, that their lunch each day was being provided by a local hotel, but any thoughts of a nice bit of pork pie and maybe a few pickles on the side, had soon turned to dust. He would have bet a bob or two that the judge would not be munching on yesterday's bread and a lump of meat which was stringy with fat. Nothing but the best for the nobs, he thought.

His solicitor Mr Hyams and his barrister Mr Streatfield had both popped in for a few minutes, bringing with them a spirit of cautious optimism and Mr Hyams had said that there was a chance that Charlie might be allowed in to see him for a few minutes. 'I've explained that your brother-in-law wishes to discuss a matter to do with the management of the case,' the solicitor said. 'So it's likely that permission will be given.'

Charlie arrived just as Ernest was attempting to rinse the last of the stale crumbs from his mouth with a mug of lukewarm tea.

'Well then,' Charlie said. 'Tea is it? I bet you can't wait to get this lot over with and sup down your first pint of ale as a free man, eh, Ernie?'

'You're not wrong.'

Ernest had stood up to take his brother-in-law's outstretched hand, but resumed his seat without making contact at a look from one of his minders. Any form of physical contact with his visitors was prohibited by regulations. Charlie too got the message and retracted the hand before dropping into a vacant chair which faced his wife's brother across the table that filled most of the room.

'We haven't but a few minutes so I'll get straight to the point,' Charlie said. 'Some of us are a bit surprised that we're not to be called as witnesses. We've all made statements about what went on in June, as you know. Me and Doris, and your Ma and all.'

'I know you have. I appreciate it, I really do.'

'I asked Mr Hyams why we weren't to give evidence after all and he said it's on account of this barrister bloke.'

'That's right. You see Charlie, Mr Streatfield is the one what decides how best to run my case.'

'I see.' Charlie paused to think about it, as if he didn't really see at all. 'But surely Ernest, he must know that what we can swear to is important. It proves that Dolly Morton isn't telling the truth about what happened in June – and if she isn't telling the truth about that, then she probably isn't telling the truth about a lot of other things too. Why, the jury must surely have known that! All that stuff about you hitting her and kicking her. Where were the bruises then, I should like to know, and why didn't Freddie Morton ever notice them? Or any of her other fancy men, come to that.'

'The jury will see right through all that,' said Ernest, but he was suddenly aware that his voice lacked conviction. The jury were a mystery to him, an unknown quantity. The truth was that he did not know what they were thinking at all.

'How about Kathleen Holmes then? She worked there for two years and could tell them a thing or two about Dolly Morton's carryings on *and* she knew all about the ins and outs of it between you and her and all.'

'Mr Hyams is still trying to find her.'

'If only you could remember the name of the place where she went to,' Charlie said.

'Aye, well I didn't take that much notice at the time. Cooks and house maids come and go. I mean I always got on all right with the lass, but I can't say as we were ever all that friendly. Not so's you'd write to one another or expect to keep in touch. Not with her moving down south.'

'Perhaps if you was to advertise in the papers for her?'

'Oh aye,' Ernest said sarcastically. 'I'll just place a call to my stockbroker and rustle up the ready cash. Have you any idea what it costs to place an advertisement in the national newspapers?'

'Sorry Ernest. I wasn't thinking.'

'That's all right. Even if Mr Hyams doesn't find her, we've right on our side, and that's the main thing, isn't it?'

'Of course it is,' Charlie agreed. 'But even so, I think you should maybe have another word with that barrister of yours. See if you can't persuade him to call us lot as witnesses.'

'It's almost time to go back up now,' warned the taller of the two warders.

'I'll mention it to him again,' Ernest promised. 'Give Ma and the girls a hug for me, will you? Tell them to keep their chins up. And all the best to Dad – and Charlie—' the four occupants of the cell had all risen to their feet by now and Charlie was already being ushered politely but firmly out of the door, '—give Ethel a kiss and tell her that her Daddy will soon be home to see her.'

'I will Ernest. I will.'

Charlie disappeared down the corridor and Ernest found himself being walked back towards the stairs which led straight up into the dock. The court had already begun to look familiar. It seemed that everyone but him and the judge was already in his or her allotted place. Now it wanted only for the arrival of the ring master, he thought, before the show could recommence.

CHAPTER SIX

Tuesday 12 December 1933
Leeds Town Hall, The Yorkshire Assizes

After the adjournment, the chief witness for the prosecution was back in the box. Ernest studied her closely, but Dolly showed no outward signs of discomfiture or distress. Her chin was tilted upward, her expression calm, her voice as level and confident as if she were the lady mayoress, presenting the prizes on speech day.

'I'm going to move now to the evening and night of your husband's death,' said Mr Streatfield. 'I think you have told us that when Brown initially returned to the farm that night, you were out in the yard, filling a bucket at the water trough?'

'That is correct.'

'So... Brown stopped the horsebox in the yard, got down from the driver's seat and told you that he had brought back a cow, which had been turned away by one of your husband's customers?'

'No. He told me that much later.'

'You are sure that he did not tell you immediately?'

'Absolutely sure.'

'Your husband was a cattle factor, wasn't he?'

'Yes.'

'And this involves leasing out cattle, and selling them over a period of time, by means of payment plans.'

'It does.'

'Your husband often repossessed cattle, did he not? Sometimes as many as fifty beasts at a time?'

'I don't know. My husband handled the business, not me.'

'If a farmer couldn't pay – even if he had paid all but the very last instalment – the cattle would be repossessed, wouldn't they?'

'I don't know anything about that.'

'Farmers sometimes came to Saxton Grange to complain about the way they had been treated, didn't they?'

'I have no idea. I knew nothing of that side of the business.'

'But surely, Mrs Morton, you are a director of Cattle Factors? It says so here, on the company letterhead.'

'I repeat that I knew almost nothing of the business.'

'Your husband was a hard man, was he not? The sort of man who would make many enemies?'

'He drove a good bargain.'

'And he had made enemies?'

'Not that I know of.'

'Well,' said Mr Streatfield, his voice deceptively kind. 'Let us return to the evening of 5 September, when Ernest Brown returned with the unwanted cow. He stopped the horsebox and after some kind of brief conversation between you, you helped him get the cow into the mistal?'

'No, I didn't.'

'Ernest Brown says that you did.'

'Then he is lying.'

'Ernest Brown says that you helped him with the cow and that is how you came to be in the mistal. Whereas you say that he took hold of you, when you were alongside the horse trough and dragged you into the mistal.'

'That is correct.'

'But the mistal is on the other side of the farm yard to the trough. It's a matter of maybe twenty yards. Are you saying that he dragged you all the way across the farm yard?'

'Yes.' Dolly's voice was quietly determined.

'He did this in full view of the house, where Ann Houseman might be watching from any of the windows?'

'Yes.'

'This man was so bold that he dragged the mistress of the house across the full width of the farm yard, in full view of the house – and in particular of the kitchen window, where Miss Houseman was most likely to be, at that time of day?'

In the face of the defence barrister's sarcastic incredulity, Dorothy Morton's voice carried a quiet authority. 'That is correct.'

'Is it true that the floor of the mistal was slippery?'

'Not exceptionally.'

'And that you slipped over accidentally?'

'No.'

'Didn't Brown tell you that he wanted to get finished with his chores quickly that evening, as he intended going out again?'

'I don't remember him saying that.'

'Now, when you shouted for Miss Houseman and she came out into the yard, to see if you had called her, can you explain why you then denied having shouted her name?'

'I was afraid of Brown.'

'I see. This terrible fear you had of Brown,' Mr Streatfield lingered over the words, as if pondering them afresh. 'So you could not say anything to Miss Houseman whilst you were still out in the yard, within his hearing. But surely, once you and Miss Houseman had gone into the house, leaving Brown out in the barn, you could have told her then, about this incident in the mistal, where you say that Brown attacked you?'

'I told her about it later on.'

'Later on? Later on that same evening?'

'No.'

'Then when?'

'I told her the following morning.'

'But you were alone with Miss Houseman many times during the course of that night, why wait until the next morning to tell her?'

'I did not tell her until the next morning.'

'Yes, we know that.' Mr Streatfield attempted to press the point, but Dorothy Morton continued to respond with quiet determination. She had been terrified of Brown, she said, and this it seemed, gave ample excuse for any behaviour which might appear less than rational.

Next Mr Streatfield asked her again about the sound of cars coming down the drive. Yes, Dorothy agreed, she and Ann had been within earshot of the drive during the entire evening, and no, they had not heard any vehicle come down towards the garage until the wheels which had ground past at around eleven thirty that night. Nor had they heard any shots, save the lone volley which had been fired by Ernest Brown, close to the kitchen window at around nine thirty.

In the public gallery, the old biddies fidgeted and shrugged. They had heard all this already. It had been thoroughly gone into by Mr Paley Scott. It was overly warm inside the court room, for those still wearing their winter coats and hats. Here and there a head began to nod, though some of them perked up a bit, when Dolly was again asked to describe how she and her companion had fled into the dining room, on hearing the shot from the yard.

'Why did you run into the dining room and hide under the table?' asked Mr Streatfield. Was there the faintest edge of sarcasm in his voice? Did he perhaps think, as some of the other observers must surely have done, that this witness who stood, confident and unflinching in the face of his interrogation, did not look much like the sort of hysterical woman who would dive under a dining table at the first sign of trouble?

'We were terrified,' the witness replied patiently. 'We thought that Brown might kill us.'

'I see.' Mr Streatfield nodded, as if grateful for this elucidation. 'There was a telephone call, was there not, during the course of the evening?'

'Yes. Miss Houseman took the call. It was someone wanting to speak to my husband on a matter of business.'

'So at around nine forty or so that night, after you had heard Brown using the gun in the yard and had become convinced that he was going to kill you, you knew that the telephone was in full working order?'

'Yes.'

'Why then did you not take advantage of this call to seek some help? Or simply pick up the telephone and speak to the exchange at any time?'

'I dared not raise the alarm with the exchange as Brown could have been listening, either in the kitchen or else standing just outside the drawing room window.'

'But surely, either you, or Miss Houseman, could have got to the telephone for a moment or two, at some point during the evening?'

'No. We were constantly afraid of what Brown might do. When he wasn't in the kitchen with us, he could have been listening outside.'

'How about later on, when Brown had left the house and you and Miss Houseman had gone upstairs? You had no way of knowing that the telephone wires had been cut, had you? Why not creep downstairs then, and raise the alarm?'

'I have already told you, we were constantly in terror of meeting Brown.'

'The Essex motor car had been left at the top of the drive, had it not, when Miss Houseman brought the jam pan back to the farm?'

'That is correct.'

'So the car was standing alongside the road for the better part of the evening. Did it never occur to you to make your escape from Brown, using the car?'

'There would not have been time.'

'Then there is the matter of the knife. You have sworn that you saw Brown take the game knife – that is a knife with a white handle – out from the kitchen drawer?'

'Yes.'

Ernest noticed that one of the jurymen was gazing intently at the oak table in the well of the court, where the white handled knife lay alongside the various other exhibits; the plans of the farm, the album of photographs, a shotgun, a length of rope, and another black-handled knife.

'You are prepared to swear that Brown took a knife with a *white* handle outside, even though you have told us that the kitchen was then in darkness, except for a single paraffin lamp?'

'The lamp gave a very good level of light. It was definitely the game knife, which has a white handle.'

Mr Streatfield changed tack abruptly. 'Did you not think it strange that your husband had not returned home for his supper?'

'It was not unusual for him to come in more than two or three hours after he had said he would be home.'

'But presumably it *was* unusual for him to come home so late and then to go straight out again?'

'Yes.'

'Did you not think to ask Brown *why* your husband was going out again?'

'No. My husband would not have told Brown where he was going, as he would have thought it none of his business.'

'When you heard the car coming down the drive, you believed it to be your husband coming home, did you not?'

'Yes.'

'You must have been very relieved. Why didn't you run out onto the drive at once, to solicit his help?'

'We were afraid of meeting Brown outside, with the gun.'

'But you have already told us that Brown had cleaned the gun and put it away in the kitchen cupboard.'

'Well we were afraid of meeting him outside at all, with anything... in any circumstances.'

'But your husband was coming down the drive and you believed yourself to be in considerable peril. Surely you would naturally have rushed outside to attract his attention?'

'We did not think of it.'

'After all, you could not be sure that your husband would leave his car in the garage and then come into the kitchen, could you?'

'Well,' Dolly hesitated. 'I'm not sure that I understand what you mean.'

'It was not unknown for your husband to fall asleep at the wheel of his car, and spend the night in the garage, was it?'

'It had occurred once or twice,' she conceded reluctantly.

'So in order to be sure that your husband would come to your aid, it would have been best to have gone out into the yard, and attracted his attention?' A pause. 'Particularly if you suspected that he had spent the larger part of his evening in a local public house?'

'I had no way of knowing where he had spent his evening. I believed him to be out on business.'

'Very well. Now you say that after you had gone upstairs, you looked out of the window and saw Brown, as you put it, "creeping about the yard" and that you saw him re-enter the kitchen, after you had gone up to bed.'

'I have already said so, yes.'

'Doesn't Brown have some chores to do, last thing at night? Doesn't he have to cross the yard to stoke up the boiler? And if he should decide to fetch his jacket from the kitchen, or obtain a glass of water, or eat the supper which had been left out for him on the kitchen table, wouldn't he have to enter the kitchen, to accomplish any of those things?'

'Yes, but that isn't what he was doing.'

'I put it to you, Mrs Morton that from your position, locked in the bathroom, it would hardly be possible for you to see what Ernest Brown was doing in the kitchen.'

Ernest wondered if the jury had noticed the momentary glint of annoyance in Dolly's eyes.

On receiving no reply from the witness, Mr Streatfield moved on again. 'Tell me, is Saxton Grange an old house, Mrs Morton?'

'I suppose so.' She seemed thrown by the question.

'Isn't it well over a hundred years old?'

'I have no idea how old it is.'

'But like most old houses, the floorboards tend to creak, do they not?'

'Yes.'

'So it would be a common thing to hear the woodwork creaking at night, whether there was anyone moving about inside or not?'

'I suppose so.'

'And the cistern in the attic is also prone to making noises, I think? While you were hiding in the bathroom and later when you were with Miss Houseman, you never actually looked out onto the landing to see if it really was Brown, moving about and causing these noises, did you?'

'No, but...'

'Thank you, Mrs Morton. I want to return now to the shotgun, which was normally kept in the kitchen cupboard, was it not? Firstly, perhaps you can tell me whether or not you yourself can handle a gun?'

'I have shot rabbits. I am not an expert.'

'But even in your youth, you had a gun of your own, isn't that so?'

'Yes.'

'So unlike Miss Houseman, you are not nervous of handling a gun?'

'No.'

'When the defendant had finished cleaning the gun that night, you say that he put it back into the cupboard?'

'Yes.'

'Was the gun loaded?'

'No.'

'Where was the ammunition kept?'

'In the same cupboard.'

'Was the cupboard kept locked?'

'No.'

'Was there anything to prevent any member of the household – or indeed anyone at all who entered the kitchen – from getting hold of the gun and the cartridges?'

'Nothing at all.'

Mr Streatfield allowed the assembled listeners to consider the point, while he took another drink from his water glass. Dorothy Morton continued to give him her full attention, seemingly determined to look nowhere in court but at the defending counsel.

'There was a bang, was there not, just before you went to the window and saw that the garage was on fire?'

'Yes.'

'Was it a sound like a gunshot?'

'No, not at all. It was more of a dull thud. I believe it was associated with the fire.'

'So, you looked out of the window and saw that the garage was on fire. Why did you not shout out to Brown, for assistance?'

'I was afraid. I feared that my husband might be in the garage. I was afraid that Brown might have killed him and was going to kill me too.'

Though watching Dorothy Morton closely, Ernest remained aware of the judge. He was a pernickety old fellow, Ernest thought, and for some reason seemed particularly interested in the plans of the farm, which he was peering at again now. Every time some location had been mentioned in the evidence, he had insisted on having it indicated on the plans and periodically he returned to his complaint that the draughtsman who had drawn up the plans on behalf of the prosecution, had shown all the doorways only as openings in the walls, with no indication that they actually had any doors in them. For some reason this obscure detail appeared to trouble him much more than any of the other material facts. Now he decided to interrupt the cross examination in order to query whether or not the garage was fitted with doors. Dorothy confirmed that it was, adding that the doors would normally stand open until both cars had been put away for the night.

By now even the obsequious Mr Paley Scott had become fed up with the recurrent issue of the missing doors, and when Mr Justice Humphreys tetchily complained for the umpteenth time that, 'For some reason this fellow has not put a door in,' the prosecuting counsel said: 'Presumably my lord, the door will be found in the doorway.'

Ernest managed to suppress the desire to laugh, though one or two others in the court did not. Dolly, he noted, remained impassive.

Pretending not to notice the snub, the judge turned his attention to the woman in the witness box. 'There is something I would like you to help me with,' he said, adopting the voice of the kindly headmaster, Ernest thought, rather than Mr Streatfield's much more censorious teacher. 'Though this man had behaved, as you say, brutally towards you that evening, you did not, I think, suspect that he might harm your husband, until the shot was fired in the yard?'

'No, my lord.'

'So it was not until the shot was fired that you became really frightened.'

'I had been frightened of him for a long time.'

'But that night in particular?'

'Yes. Because he seemed like a madman.'

'I see.' The judge nodded, turning his attention from the witness box to the dock and favouring Ernest with a long, hard look, before saying: 'You may continue, Mr Streatfield.'

The defence counsel resumed as invited. 'I want to ask you about the rope which you and Mr Stuart noticed on the landing, when you returned to Saxton Grange and searched the house in the early hours of the morning,' he said.

Ernest watched as Dorothy nodded, tight lipped. The rope had already been brought into court as an exhibit and now it was carried across the room to be shown to the witness. In order to reach the defending barrister, it had to pass before the man in the dock: a rope with a loop made in one the end. It was by now late afternoon and the recently installed electric lights which had been burning all day, were beginning to cast grotesque shapes around the room. The barristers in their gowns were transformed into gigantic birds, flapping high above the heads of the jurors, the policeman at the door had become a stunted tree trunk, which lay diagonally across the wooden floor. As Mr Streatfield held the rope aloft there was a collective gasp among the spectators in the public gallery, for unbeknown to Ernest himself, and unseen by Streatfield, it had cast the shadow of a noose, suspended above the man in the dock. If Dorothy Morton was aware of the eerie symbolism, she gave no sign.

'Now you have told the court that this rope only appeared on the landing, after you and Miss Houseman had left the house, and also that Ernest Brown threatened that he would use it to strangle you, if you breathed a word of what had happened to anyone.'

'That is right.'

'I put it to you, that this story of Brown threatening you with this, or any other rope, is a complete fabrication.'

'It's the truth.'

'Mrs Morton, isn't it the case that spare rope for making halters is kept in the attic of the farmhouse?'

'Yes.'

'So there would be nothing out of the ordinary in Brown going upstairs to fetch some rope on that night or indeed on any other night, and that this is exactly what he was doing, when you and Miss Houseman met him coming downstairs, as you went to answer the telephone?'

'He was not supposed to go upstairs without asking permission.'

'I will let that pass. Can you tell me whether there was a light burning on the upstairs landing that night?'

'No. Not on the landing.'

'So if Brown had gone up to the attic and taken an armful of ropes, one of which he had inadvertently dropped on the landing, it is entirely possible that it would have gone unnoticed until you and Mr Stuart searched the house some hours later, with the benefit of a torch.'

'No. Miss Houseman or I would have seen it.'

'You cannot be definite on that point, I think. And isn't it also the case, that although you have described the rope as being left outside your bedroom door, when the police marked the plan of the house to show where the rope was found, they put it in this corner of the landing – you see it here on the plan, marked with a blue cross – and that this cross is not outside any door at all.'

'I saw it outside my door.'

'Mrs Morton, isn't this whole story of the rope being left outside your door, and of Brown telling you that he had left it there on purpose, a complete invention?'

'No. It is not.'

'You have told us that you had conceived a real hatred of Brown last summer.'

'I had hated him for a long time.'

'I suggest Mrs Morton, that you are blackening this case against Brown, in order to shield someone else. Isn't it true that there was another man with whom you were on affectionate terms last summer – a man who has a motor car and who lives less than thirty miles from Saxton Grange?'

Dorothy Morton hesitated. For a second she glanced appealingly in the direction of the judge, but realising that she would get no help from that quarter, she turned back to Streatfield. 'I have already said so.'

'Not, I think, that the man lived less than thirty miles away.'

'Not that perhaps.'

'Nor that he had a motor car.'

'Nor that.'

'I suggest that there was a second man at Saxton Grange that night, and I suggest that you know who this man is.'

'That's nonsense.' Though she had been standing in the witness box for several hours by now, neither her voice nor her demeanour betrayed the slightest sign of fatigue.

'I put it to you again that some other man came to the house that night. That it was not Brown, but some other man who cut the telephone wires, shot Frederick Morton and set fire to the garage. I suggest that you are blaming Ernest Brown, in order to shield some other person.'

Dorothy's voice slid higher up the scale as she declared, 'Nobody else came near the house that night at all.'

At this point old Humphreys intervened again. For a moment Ernest wondered if it would be some irrelevant point regarding the blue cross on the plan and the lack of bedroom doors marked thereon, but instead it was to suggest that if Mr Streatfield had a particular person in mind, then he should put the name to Mrs Morton and give her the opportunity of confirming or denying it.

'I'm afraid that isn't possible, my lord.'

'But I understood you to be identifying a particular person: someone with whom Mrs Morton was on close terms of friendship and who might therefore be assumed to be antagonistic toward her husband.'

'Yes, my lord,' said Mr Streatfield. 'That is the kind of possibility I had in mind. I am obliged to your lordship for raising the question.'

'If you can identify this person, Mr Streatfield, then all of Yorkshire, if necessary all of England will be scoured in order to bring him here.' Travers Humphreys glared expectantly at the defending counsel, who had begun to look discomfited and took a couple of sips from his ever ready glass of water.

'I'm afraid that I cannot identify him, my lord.'

'You are not then, specifically pointing a finger in the direction of this one particular man?'

'My lord, only Mrs Morton can tell us if such a person was there that night.'

'So you are suggesting that Mrs Morton knows perfectly well who this person is, and whether or not he was present at the farm that night?'

To Ernest's horror, Streatfield began to flounder slightly. 'It is going to be suggested that it is *a possibility*.'

'That Mrs Morton knows to whom you refer, or that the man to whom you refer was at the house that night?' The judge appeared to be genuinely confused.

Mr Paley Scott took this as an opportunity to clamber to his feet and ask a long string of questions about this hypothetical, unnamed man, which – since Mr Streatfield could not answer any of them – swiftly had the desired effect upon the judge's patience. 'Need we pursue this any further, Mr Streatfield? You seem to be heading off in an extremely speculative direction. You are suggesting, I think, that this mysterious man might have been a lover, or an ex-lover, or a poacher, or a man who was unhappy about a business matter, or indeed any human being that you care to mention, but apparently there is no clear idea that this man ever existed at all.'

Mr Streatfield conceded defeat. He had no further questions for the witness. Dorothy Morton left the stand. Tall, slim, elegantly clad in her dark suit and her little fur, she passed within feet of the man who had once been her lover, glancing neither right nor left, with her head held high.

'Look at me, Dolly,' he willed her. 'Look at me, damn you.' But she did not turn her head.

CHAPTER SEVEN

Tuesday 12 December 1933
Leeds Town Hall, The Yorkshire Assizes

'The court calls Miss Ann Houseman.'

Like her employer, Ann Houseman walked directly in front of the dock, without so much as glancing at the man who sat inside it. She took the oath in a clear, rather piping voice, then focussed all her attention on Mr Paley Scott. Yes, she said, in answer to his initial questions, she was a nurse maid and companion, and had been employed at Saxton Grange since July that year.

Ernest sat in the dock, watching her closely. She was trying to ape Dolly, he thought. Very aware that all eyes were upon her. Very aware of her considerable importance in the grand scheme of things. It didn't quite come off though. She wasn't a lady and she hadn't the maturity. Silly little chit. Companion indeed! Companions were drawn from the ranks of distressed gentlefolk, not young lasses like herself, with one brother a bus conductor and another labouring on a farm. If Dorothy had been like the grand lady, giving out the speech day prizes, then Ann Houseman was a shoe-in for the part of the overly eager Head Girl, reciting a carefully memorised speech of welcome, prior to dropping a curtsey and handing over a bunch of flowers.

'So, Miss Houseman, you only joined the household after Brown had been reinstated in June?'

'Yes.'

'Now Miss Houseman, I want you tell us in your own words, what happened on that fateful evening in September. You had been sent on an errand to fetch a jam pan, had you not?' Mr Paley Scott prompted, using his gentle, guiding voice.

'That's right. I went out in the Essex motor car. I was only away from the house for about half an hour. I left at about seven thirty and got back at about eight o'clock. I left the car at the top of the drive as usual, walked down the drive – it's only a few yards – then went straight into the house with the pan, to start on the jam-making. The next thing I specifically remember was hearing Mrs Morton, calling out "Ann, Ann!"'

The witness paused but on receiving a nod of encouragement from the prosecuting counsel, she continued: 'I went into the yard to see what the matter was and as I crossed it, I saw Mrs Morton, coming out of the barn. She seemed frightened, but when I asked her if she'd called me, she said "no". We went back to the house together, but I went back into the kitchen and she went straight upstairs.'

'And did you see Brown at this time?'

'Not then, but the horse box was back in the yard, so I knew that he must have returned and I guessed that he must be in the barn or something.'

'And when did you first see him that evening?'

'He came into the kitchen a few minutes later. He looked quite wild. He said he wanted to see Mrs Morton, so I ran upstairs to fetch her, but she said she couldn't come down just then. She was obviously frightened and didn't want to see the man, Brown. I could tell that there was something wrong.'

'What did Mrs Morton actually say to you?'

'Mrs Morton said that she would be down in a few minutes, so I went back to the kitchen and continued boiling the fruit. I told Brown that Mrs Morton was coming and he stood waiting for her. Eventually she came downstairs, but instead of telling her anything urgent, he just told her about a cow he had brought back from Greetland and then he went outside again.'

'And then what happened?'

'A little while later – by now it was probably nine o'clock – he came in again and asked Mrs Morton if she would help him put the ducks away, but she told him that she couldn't, as she was waiting for a phone call from her father.'

'And was she in fact waiting for a phone call?'

'No. She just said it as an excuse.'

'Thank you. Pray continue.'

'Brown went out on his own again. It was about half an hour after that when we heard the shot.'

'Did it seem to you to have been fired from somewhere close at hand?'

'Oh yes. It sounded as if the pellets had hit the kitchen window. Mrs Morton and I both cried out and ran towards the front of the house. Mrs Morton hid under the dining room table and I went back to the kitchen. Brown was already back inside and I asked him what he had been shooting at, and he said, "a rat".'

'Did he have the gun with him when he came into the kitchen?' enquired Mr Paley Scott.

'No, not then.'

'And what took place after that?'

'He went back outside and after a few minutes Mrs Morton came back into the kitchen and got out her sewing, and I was carrying on with the jam. It was dark by then, so I drew the curtains and lit a paraffin lamp. Mrs Morton sat near it, so that she could see to do her sewing. Then the telephone rang and we both rushed to answer it. As we crossed the hall, we saw Brown, coming downstairs.'

'Did you speak to him?'

'No. We were both too afraid to speak to him. I answered the phone. It was a long distance call from Scotland, asking for Mr Morton. I said he was not at home, but was expected back at any time and I suggested that they should call back in about fifteen minutes. After that we went back into the kitchen and Brown came in again soon afterwards and took something from the knife drawer and went straight back outside with it.'

'Did you see what it was?'

'No. Only that he took something from the drawer and then returned with it a few minutes later and put it back. Then he went outside again and a couple of minutes later he came back in with the gun. He laid the gun on the dresser and said to me, "You go, as I want to speak to Mrs Morton alone."'

Ernest wondered if everyone else had noticed the way the girl drew herself up, and gave a little theatrical pause in readiness for her big moment.

'I said, "I will not go out. If you have anything to say to Mrs Morton, you can say it in front of me." Then he said, "No, I can't do that. It will be much better for you, if you go out." He picked up the gun, and I said, "You had better give me that gun," but he refused... Then he offered it to me, but I wouldn't take it.' The young woman's voice dropped at the admission.

Not quite so brave after all, Ernest thought.

'I didn't have time to take it from him,' the witness continued, 'because he snatched it back, when I reached out my hand. After that he began to clean the gun.'

Ernest did a double take at this new addition to the evidence. At the magistrates' court, she had simply admitted to being afraid to take hold of the gun, but Ann Houseman now seemed intent on embellishing her role as the heroine of the piece.

'Did you notice anything about the gun? How many cartridges remained in it, for example?' asked the prosecution counsel.

'No. He took the gun apart and cleaned it, piece by piece, but I wasn't really paying that much attention, because I had to carry on watching the jam. When he had finished, he put the gun away in the cupboard and went out again. He came back in soon afterwards, with the big dog and sat down at the kitchen table. Mrs Morton said to him, "Some people have been ringing up from Scotland, asking for Mr Morton," and he said, "The phone hasn't been ringing lately."'

'And after that?'

'We all sat talking. He kept hinting that I should go to bed and making the big dog growl at me.' Just for a second, she darted a look across at the man in the dock. It was a look of pure loathing.

She had always been afraid of that dog, Ernest thought. She was a thoroughly silly, prissy kind of girl, not at all suited to a life out in the country.

'I said that I couldn't leave the jam,' she continued. 'Eventually, at about eleven, Brown went outside again. He had been gone for some time when we heard a car pass the kitchen window: it was going down the drive in the direction of the garage. Mrs Morton and I were listening intently, of course, because we were constantly expecting Mr Morton to come home.'

'And after you had heard the car?' prompted Mr Paley Scott.

'Soon after we heard the car, Brown came back into the kitchen and Mrs Morton said, "Was that the Chrysler?" and Brown said, "Yes. The boss has been in and he's gone out again".'

'And had you heard the sound of a car going back up the drive in the opposite direction?'

'No. I had not heard any sound of a car turning, or going back up the drive.'

'And how did Brown seem at this time.'

The witness darted another quick look at the man in the box. 'He seemed bold and at his ease,' her voice said, while her eyes said, but he's not sitting so easy now.

'So you continued to sit there together – the three of you, in the kitchen?'

'Yes. We stayed there until it was nearly midnight, then Mrs Morton and I went up to bed. I knew that she had gone into the bathroom, and I did not undress, but stayed at my bedroom window. At about half past midnight I saw Brown again, moving about in the yard.

He looked up at my window and saw me standing there, and he glared up at me. Then he unlocked the kitchen door with his key and came back into the house. This made me so afraid that I went and joined Mrs Morton in the bathroom. After that we heard the boards creaking, as Brown moved about the house. Later on we went to sit on the bed in my bedroom and the same thing happened, while we waited together in there.'

'And what did you do then?'

'We didn't do anything. We sat on the bed, too frightened to get undressed. We just stayed there talking quietly and listening for Brown moving about, until eventually we heard the crackling noises, and Mrs Morton looked out of the window and saw that the garage was on fire.'

Ernest listened carefully as the girl repeated the story of their subsequent flight to Towton. Unlike Dolly, she had not returned to Saxton Grange immediately, but had stayed at the Stuart's house, taking care of the still sleeping baby, Diana, until he himself had been sent to fetch her back to the farm at around seven in the morning. He could picture it all clearly. A low sun rising in the pale blue sky as they drove past the stubble fields, coming at last level with the orchard, where the apples were still ripening on the trees. He remembered how she had sat alongside him in the front of the horsebox, with the baby in her lap, not speaking a word to him – fancying herself, as she always had, a cut above the mere farm labourers, but gasping aloud when they came in sight of the smoking ruins which represented what was left of the garage and some of the outbuildings.

'At what time approximately did you return to the farm?' asked Mr Paley Scott.

'It was about seven o'clock in the morning. When I saw what awful devastation had occurred to the garage, I made some sort of exclamation, and Brown said, "Isn't it terrible? I'm afraid the boss must be in it." Then he gave me a threatening look.'

'And did you have any further conversation with Brown that morning?'

'Yes. At around eleven o'clock I went up to Brown and asked him what had happened when he had seen Mr Morton the night before, and he told me that Mr Morton was drunk when he got home and was racing the engine of the Chrysler.'

'And had you heard the engine racing, the night before?'

'No, I had not. The car had freewheeled down the drive and I had not heard the sound of an engine at all.'

The December afternoon had closed in, darkening the big skylights upon which the court relied for natural illumination. During a pause in the evidence, it had been possible to make out the voices of some carol singers, youngsters by the sound of it, working their way through *Once in Royal David's City*. The electric lights had been burning all day long, but now they were making the brass railing glow across the front of the dock, and reflecting off the gold topped pen on the judge's bench. 'You'll be back home in time for Christmas,' his brother-in-law, Charlie, had said, during his last visit to the prison. The youthful voices of the carollers reminded him of Ethel, at home in Huddersfield, dreaming of Father Christmas. Ma said she was hoping for a new doll.

A flurry of hailstones pelted against the ceiling glass, just as Mr Streatfield stood up to take his turn at questioning the witness.

'Now, Miss Houseman, I want to ask you to tell us a little more about that evening, in the kitchen. Were you really terrified of Mr Brown the whole of that time?'

The young woman hesitated. 'Not the whole time, no.'

'For example, when Brown initially entered the kitchen that night and asked you to fetch Mrs Morton down from the nursery, because he had something that he wished to speak with her about, did you have any reason to be afraid of him then?'

'No. Not then, though Mrs Morton seemed to be distressed and a bit frightened.'

'How about later on, when Ernest Brown asked you to leave the room, so that he could speak with Mrs Morton alone, were you very afraid of him then?'

'Not so much then. But Mrs Morton was very afraid of him. She asked me not to go.'

'I am not asking you to tell us about your impression of Mrs Morton. What about when you asked him to hand you the gun? Were you afraid of him then?'

'I was afraid then, yes.'

'And you asked him for the gun, but you did not take it?'

'No, I was afraid.'

'You did not take the gun because you were afraid? So it is not fair to say, as you did a little while ago, that you would have taken it, except that it was snatched away too quickly?'

'No.' Her head drooped like a snowdrop: a child caught out in a fib.

'Now you have told the court that you did not go upstairs that night until almost midnight. During this long evening of sitting in the kitchen, you did not sit in silence, did you?'

'No. We had the wireless on.'

'And as well as the wireless, you had some conversation, did you not?'

'Some, yes.'

'Conversation between all three of you?'

'Yes.'

'What was Mr Brown talking about, during this time?'

'Well,' the witness hesitated again, as if surprised by the question. 'Just about the horses and the farm. Normal things.'

'So, he was able to talk in an ordinary way, about ordinary things?'

'Not in an ordinary way. He looked wild… mad.'

'And yet what he said about the horses and cattle and so on, was perfectly ordinary and sensible, was it not?'

'Yes.'

'When Mrs Morton made her remark about the telephone call from Scotland, I put it to you that your recollection is slightly at fault... Didn't Brown merely say, "Have they?" when Mrs Morton told him that someone had rung up?'

'No.'

'And even if he did say something to the effect that he had not heard the telephone ringing for some time, it was no more than the truth, was it?'

The witness's cheeks had lost their colour. The Head Girl was vanishing before their eyes.

'Was it?' Mr Streatfield repeated. 'Because the telephone had not rung for some time, had it?'

'No.' There was no disguising the young woman's petulance. Surely, Ernest thought, a point for our side.

'You say that you had become very afraid of Ernest Brown during the course of the evening, and yet you did not attempt to use the telephone, to summon help. Why was that?'

'We were too afraid. We didn't know where Brown was, from one minute to the next.'

'Ah yes. You had seen him coming downstairs from the attic, I think. Did you know that spare ropes were kept up in the attic?'

'No. I've never been in the attic, I don't know what's kept up there.'

'When you saw Ernest Brown descending the stairs, did you not see what he was carrying?'

'I didn't notice whether he was carrying anything or not.'

'So it is quite possible that he was in fact carrying some ropes?' When he received no response, Mr Streatfield returned to pursue his original line of questioning. 'Surely, if you felt the need to obtain some help, you could have got to the telephone at some point? Could not one of you have kept watch while the other made the call? Just one word to the operator would have been enough, wouldn't it?'

'The exchange are always very slow in answering.'

'But once you got through to the exchange, it would have taken only seconds to summon some assistance?'

'When we telephone from Saxton Grange we sometimes have to wait quite a long time before we get any answer from the exchange at all.'

'Now at various times, Miss Houseman, you have described how the defendant appeared to you that night. He seemed "wild", you have said, and "mad" and yet he was also "bold and at his ease". Can you explain how he can have been all these things at once?'

The young woman hesitated. 'Well he did not show any signs of going to bed. He looked as if he was going to stay in the kitchen all night.'

'He did not show any signs of going to bed?' The barrister repeated the words, as if in incredulity. 'Is that what you call "looking mad"?'

'No. He had a wild look about him, the whole time.'

'Yet you have said that he was talking normally, about quite ordinary things.'

'Well yes,' she said, a shade desperately. 'When he was talking about general things, he was … sort of… ordinary… But if you looked at him, you could see that he was, well… wild.'

'But his voice was ordinary, and his conversation was ordinary?'

'Yes.'

'And his clothing and his hair, they were not disarranged in any way?'

'No.' It was a reluctant concession.

'Was it dark that night, by the time you went up to bed?'

'Oh yes, it was midnight or soon afterwards.'

'Are there any lights in the farm yard at night?'

'No.'

'When you watched from your bedroom window and saw Ernest Brown approaching the house, was he carrying a torch or a lantern?'

'No.'

'How then, were you able to see the expression on his face?'

The young woman in the witness box made no reply.

'Now Miss Houseman, I think you have told us that from your bedroom window, you observed Ernest Brown re-enter the kitchen, after you had gone to bed? But is it not the case that your bedroom is directly above the kitchen and therefore that from your bedroom window, it is not possible to actually see the kitchen door at all?'

'Well, you can see if someone approaches the kitchen door.'

'But not the actual door itself, I think. Miss Houseman, did you actually see this man come back into the house, after you had gone upstairs to your bedroom, or hear any actual distinct footsteps on the landing, or the stairs?'

'Well it sounded like footsteps.'

'Are you prepared to swear that you heard footsteps inside the house that night?' thundered the defending counsel.

'No.'

'Thank you, Miss Houseman.' Mr Streatfield turned to Travers Humphreys and with the words: 'I have no further questions for this witness my lord,' he swept back to his seat, leaving the girl to creep meekly from the box, a figure somewhat diminished from the confident one which had entered it earlier.

CHAPTER EIGHT

Wednesday 13 December 1933
Leeds Town Hall, The Yorkshire Assizes

Mrs Hendrie, the wife of a Galston cattle dealer, had come all the way from Ayrshire to testify, but the court did not detain her for long. Mr Paley Scott merely asked her to confirm what had occurred when she had tried to telephone Mr Frederick Morton regarding a matter of business, on Tuesday 5 September. When Mr Streatfield announced that he had no questions for her at all, Mrs Hendrie seemed almost disappointed. It was such a dull little tale of how she had asked the operator to connect the call and how he had come back on the line a moment or two later, to tell her that Mr Morton was not at home, but would probably be back in about fifteen minutes; a transaction which had been followed up with a second attempt to connect the call, after which the operator had told her that there was now no reply from Mr Morton's number at all.

Mrs Hendrie was followed into the witness box by a succession of telephone operators from the exchanges which had been needed to route the call across the border and along the line to Saxton Grange, each taking their turn to trace these abortive attempts at communication for the benefit of the judge and jury. John Clarke, represented the Glasgow exchange, James McKenzie spoke up for Leeds, while Mary Morris took to the field for the little telephone office at Tadcaster. They all agreed that the first call had been placed at nine forty, and that the second – unanswered – call had been made at ten o'clock. Mary Morris provided the additional information that she had unsuccessfully attempted to connect another caller to Saxton Grange that night. This had been a purely local call, emanating from the telephone booth in Tadcaster Market Place, which had been made at ten minutes to eleven that night, but two separate attempts had failed to raise a response on that occasion.

Julius Whitehead, a telephone linesman, rounded off the evidence about the telephone, by confirming that on the morning following these abortive attempts to contact the farm, he had inspected the wires leading to the telephone which was located inside the house at Saxton Grange, and found that they had been cut, at a point just outside the drawing room window. Whitehead then explained, with the aid of a diagram, the way in which there were actually two lines connecting Saxton Grange to the outside world, one of which ran into the farm office, which stood on the opposite side of the drive to the main buildings and a second line which served the telephone in the drawing room. He explained that although these lines had two separate numbers, and operated entirely independently during the working day, with one number ringing out in the office and the other in the house, when the office was locked up at night, the line which served it would always be switched over so that it rang out in the house. This meant that whichever number was dialled after office hours, all the calls would be diverted to the drawing room telephone.

'So, Mr Whitehead, when the telephone line going into the house was cut that night, am I right to say that whichever number was called, the telephone would not ring out anywhere on the premises?' Mr Streatfield wanted to know.

'That's correct.'

'How about outgoing calls?'

'You can't make a call once the line's been cut.' Whitehead made no attempt to hide the fact that he thought this was a particularly stupid question.

'But the line leading into the farm office had not been cut, had it?'

'No. You could still make an outgoing call using the phone in the office.'

'Mr Whitehead, pardon me for labouring this point – you are quite definite that although the wire leading into the house had been cut, and all incoming calls had been diverted to the telephone in the drawing room, there would have been nothing at all to prevent anyone from making an outgoing call from the telephone in farm office?'

'Nothing at all,' replied the witness. 'In fact several calls were made from the office on Wednesday 6 September, before the wires running into the house were repaired.'

Ernest nodded imperceptibly. Like his barrister, he had no dispute with anything the telephone company employees had to say. However, his face hardened slightly at the name of the next witness. There was no love lost between himself and the farm bailiff. Murray Stuart had never liked him from the first. Jealousy, probably, because he, Ernest, had been longer at Saxton Grange than Stuart himself and because he had a way with the local girls and a manner that Stuart had always covertly disapproved of. He was old school, was Stuart, Ernest thought. Stood up smart when spoken too, whereas Ernest had never been one to tug his forelock. Stuart would never keep his hands in his pockets, while he spoke to his employer, nor yet answer back.

It was evident to all that Murray Stuart was uncomfortable from the moment he entered the court. A bloke like Stuart was well enough, ordering a lad to muck out the pig sties, or seeing to the gangers who'd come with the threshing machine, Ernest thought, but in among these posh folk, with their wigs and gowns and books and whatnot, he was well and truly out of his depth.

He had not expected to get any help from Stuart, which was just as well.

Once Stuart's credentials regarding the farm had been established, prosecuting counsel got straight to the point. Had the man, Brown, ever threatened to do things to Mr Morton, Mr Paley Scott wanted to know.

'Oh yes, plenty of times.'

'Can you give us any examples?'

'Well...' Stuart paused. When the words finally emerged, they came out in a rush. 'He said once, "I will clout the little bugger, one of these nights."'

'And did the accused man, Brown, come into your cottage and make threats against Mr Frederick Morton, around about July, last year?'

'He did.' Stuart sounded a little more confident in his surroundings now. He took a breath before speaking, so as not to gabble this time. 'In August last year, he came to my cottage in Towton at around midnight. He said the way things were going, we'd all be out of a job in a couple of months. He said that he could wreck the place if he wanted to – and that he would do it too.'

Ernest kept his features rigid. He and Stuart had no more than tolerated one another, but who would have expected a fellow worker to rat on a man; floating conversations in which they had engaged after a night in the pub together?

By the time Paley Scott moved on to ask about the night of the fire, Murray Stuart had warmed to his task. Brown had driven into the village at around three in the morning, the farm bailiff said, sounding the horn of the horsebox as he came, which was what had initially woken everyone. He had brought the vehicle to a halt immediately outside Stuart's own cottage and when Stuart had poked his head out of the bedroom window, in readiness to ask what the hell was going on, Brown had pre-empted the enquiry by shouting up that Saxton Grange was ablaze.

'Did you ask him whether he had phoned the fire brigade?'

'I did. He said "our phone's wrong" or "our phone's out of order". Just then I saw Ben Robinson stick his head out of his cottage door, trying to see what all the ruckus was about, so I shouted to him to run over to Mr Hall's, where they have a telephone, and call out the fire brigade. Then I went downstairs and drove back to the farm with Brown.'

'And did you ask him about Mr Morton?' prompted Paley Scott.

'Aye. Though not until we'd reached the farm gate. Then I asked him where the boss was and he said he didn't know. I also asked him where the women folk was to, and he said that he'd heard them shouting and screaming and that they must have fled.'

'Can you tell us something about Ernest Brown's appearance that night? Did he appear dishevelled perhaps, as if he had thrown on his clothes in a hurry?'

'No. He looked neat and tidy.'

'Not at all like a man who has just got out of bed in a hurry?'

'No. His tie was straight and his hair was combed flat.'

'Thank you. And can you describe what you saw when you reached Saxton Grange?'

'It was a big blaze. We couldn't get near, the heat was so intense. The roofs of both the garage and the barn had fallen in, but I thought I could see the outline of a car in the garage and I said, "I'm afraid that Mr Morton is in there."'

'And what did Brown reply?'

'He said, "By God, if he is, then nobody will ever see him again."'

'Then what did you do?'

'Well there wasn't much as we could do, just the two of us alone, so we went back to the village, to fetch Constable Broadhead. On the way back I asked Brown when he'd last seen Mr Morton, and he said that he'd last seen him at about eleven thirty, when the boss had driven himself home.' Stuart hesitated, but on receiving a nod of encouragement from counsel he went on: 'He said that he'd met Mr Morton on the drive and told him about a heifer what he'd brought back from Greetland, and then he'd asked if he should put the car away, but Mr Morton had said not, as he might be going out again. I asked if the boss had gone back out, but Brown told me that he'd gone straight to bed after that, so he didn't know whether Mr Morton had gone out again or not.'

'Did he say anything else about Mr Morton?'

'Yes. He said that when he'd seen him at half past eleven, he was "clever side out".'

From his elevated position on the bench, Travers Humphreys sounded an irritable note. 'What side? What was he talking about?'

Stuart paused, confounded, looking first at the judge, and then at Mr Paley Scott.

The prosecution counsel adopted his most helpful tone. 'The witness said he was "clever side out", my lord. I believe it is an expression intended to suggest that Mr Morton had been drinking and was perhaps, the worse for drink.'

'I see.' The judge gave a disapproving sniff.

The upper classes were always snooty about drink, Ernest thought. Or rather they were always snooty about it where others were concerned. Didn't mind getting plastered themselves of course, but woe betide anyone born without a silver spoon in his gob who had over-indulged. He could clearly recall the face of the magistrate who had once pontificated on the subject when fining him for being drunk and disorderly, the fellow's scarlet and purple nose proclaiming him to all the world for an imbiber and a hypocrite.

When it was Mr Streatfield's turn to put questions, he strode purposefully toward the witness box, clearly intending business. 'Now then, Mr Stuart. I believe you sometimes accompanied Mr Morton on his trips to the cattle markets, isn't that so?'

'Aye, it is.'

'When it came to buying stock, did Mr Morton ever take your advice on anything?'

'I can't say that he did. Mr Morton liked to make his own decisions.'

'Did you always agree with his decisions?'

'It wasn't for me to say.'

'I am asking whether you agreed with everything he did – in the line of his business?'

Stuart hesitated. His voice dropped a little as he said: 'No. Not everything.'

'And presumably if you did not always see wisdom in every decision made by Mr Morton, you would think it reasonable for other employees to hold similar opinions?'

Stuart opened his mouth then closed it again. Ernest noted that his hands rested a little more heavily on the polished front of the witness box.

'Isn't it the case, Mr Stuart that a group of you from the farm once got into a discussion, while you were drinking in the Crooked Billet public house, during which you said that you were Mr Morton's longest serving employee?'

'I may have done.' The farm bailiff's responses had become extremely cautious again.

'Come now, Mr Stuart. Didn't you say that you had worked longer at Saxton Grange than anyone else and didn't Mr Morton correct you and say, "No, Ernest has worked for me the longest"?'

'I think it happened as you say.'

'Quite so. Now isn't it the case that Ernest Brown sometimes travelled on these trips to cattle markets with Mr Morton?'

'Aye, sometimes he did.'

'Was Mr Morton friendly with Ernest Brown? Fond of him, even?'

'I really couldn't say.' The farm bailiff's customary flush had deepened.

'Did you ever hear Mr Morton complain regarding Ernest Brown?'

'I can't remember anything.'

'And he generally addressed him by his Christian name?'

'Yes.'

'Now as for these remarks which you say that you heard Ernest Brown make about Mr Morton, was that comment about clouting the little bugger the strongest thing he ever said?'

'Yes.'

'And surely,' Mr Streatfield's voice was smooth as silk. 'You didn't take that as a serious threat?'

'Yes,' said the witness firmly. 'I did.'

'Really?'

'Yes.' Stuart was so emphatic that his voice rose almost to a shout.

'Have you never heard people – particularly after they have had a drink or two – saying, "I will swipe him one" or "I will clout him"?'

'Not in that manner, no.'

'Have you never made similar remarks yourself, when someone has annoyed you in some way, not meaning them in the least.'

'No.'

'Come now, Mr Stuart. Isn't there a particular man from a neighbouring farm, of whom you would sometimes say, "I'll have him one of these days?"'

'Possibly.'

'So you have made threats yourself about people without meaning them?'

'No,' Stuart said stubbornly. 'Not like that.'

'You are telling the court that you never lose your temper and you never make rash, or hasty remarks, not even after a few drinks?'

'No.' The farm bailiff's stiff Sunday collar appeared to be pinching ever tighter, reddening his neck.

'Now, you have already told us that you did not always agree with the decisions made by Mr Morton.'

'That's right.' Stuart spoke reluctantly, perhaps sensing another trap.

'Would it surprise you that Ernest Brown did not always agree with these decisions either?'

'Not in the least.'

'Now I suggest to you that you may have misheard, or misunderstood that comment of Brown's, to the effect that you would all be out of work in a couple of months?'

'I understood it perfectly.'

'I put it to you that what Brown actually said was that Mr Frederick Morton could wreck the business and put you all out of work in a couple of months.'

Stuart shook his head. 'I didn't misunderstand.'

Bastard. Ernest silently framed the word in his mind. He wondered whether Mr Streatfield would do anything to remind the court that Murray Stuart still worked at Saxton Grange and therefore owed his living to Dorothy Morton, but the barrister had moved on again.

'When you and Brown stood at the farm gates, looking down on the burning buildings, it was you, was it not, who first suggested that Mr Morton might be inside the blazing car?'

'Yes.'

'Why did you think that?'

'I don't know.'

'Now you mentioned in your evidence that Brown appeared to be fully dressed? That his hair was neat, and so on, and that from this, you concluded that he had not been to bed.'

'That's right.'

'When you were first awakened and looked out of your window, to find Ernest Brown out in the village street, it was dark, was it not?'

'Yes.' Stuart sounded hesitant, as if uncertain where this might be leading.

'And having learned from Brown that the farm was on fire, you pulled your head back inside, threw on some clothes and went down to join him, where he was waiting for you in the horsebox – is that not so?'

'Aye. Yes. That's correct.'

'Would it be fair to say, that during the few minutes when you were putting on your own clothes, Brown, while waiting in the horse box, would have had ample opportunity to tidy up his appearance, straighten his clothing and run his fingers through his hair?'

The farm bailiff glanced across first at the prosecuting counsel, and then up at the judge himself, before admitting in a voice of plain reluctance, 'I suppose so, yes.'

CHAPTER NINE

Wednesday 13 December 1933
Leeds Town Hall, The Yorkshire Assizes

The next group of witnesses were the ones which Mr Streatfield had referred to as 'the experts', during one of those periods when he had come to talk with Ernest, while he was locked in the cells beneath the courtroom, waiting for the proceedings to begin. In times gone by, Ernest had always marvelled at the Leeds Town Hall, its palatial structure, the impressive clock tower which dwarfed everything else around it, but once inside the building, the court room itself had been smaller than he had expected, not full of columns and carvings and grandeur, but mere plain wood and plaster, which while not unpleasing on the eye, somehow failed to live up to the expectations which had been generated by the impressive façade. As for the rabbit warren of basement cells, they were just small and mean. In many ways it was like Armley jail, he thought, all got up to look like some sort of royal castle, but singularly lacking in accommodation that was fit for a king. There was no doubting the truth of his father's old adage: You can't judge a book by its cover.

The first of these expert witnesses was a man named Robert Churchill, who hardly needed any prompting from Mr Paley Scott, in his enthusiasm to describe the workings of the shotgun, which had been brought from the farm and now lay upon the table, alongside all the other exhibits. Between them, Mr Paley Scot and Mr Churchill wasted no time in setting out a scenario in which Ernest Brown could have taken the shotgun from the cupboard, fired one cartridge into Freddie Morton and the other in the yard, then cleaned the gun and replaced it in the cupboard; but once Mr Streatfield got to work, he soon had Mr Churchill admitting that although the shot found in Freddie Morton's body *could* have come from one of the Grand Prix cartridges which were kept in the kitchen cupboard, and *might* have been fired from the self-same gun which had been brought into court, it was impossible to say that this had definitely been the ammunition used, or even that the weapon from the kitchen cupboard had been the gun which fired it.

After Robert Churchill came Professor Frederick Tryhorn, of Hull University, who had come along to tell the court about some experiments he had made with the Saxton Grange telephone wires. According to the professor, when you looked at the cutting edge of the white handled knife with the naked eye, it appeared to be a single smooth blade, but when you put that same blade under a microscope, it was possible to make out a series of serrations, like those on a saw. These, the professor explained, would leave a series of distinctive scratch marks on the cut ends of the metal telephone wire, and these marks could also be seen and indeed photographed by using a microscope. It was, he said, like a fingerprint. He had been given the two different knives which the police had recovered from Saxton Grange, and he had experimented with each of them, cutting through pieces of telephone wire which were identical in every respect to the wire which had been cut outside the drawing room window.

'Can you identify these knives for us, please Professor?'

Ernest had noticed the way Mr Paley Scott liked to keep drawing everyone's attention to the things on the table, as if their very being there, somehow proved something against the man in the dock.

'They are the two knives on the table.' Professor Tryhorn indicated with a pointing finger.

'One is the white handled knife, which the police discovered in a wheelbarrow in the farm yard on the morning after the fire and the other is the black handled knife which they recovered from a kitchen drawer,' prompted Mr Paley Scott.

'That is correct. I used each knife to cut the sample telephone wire in different places, then took photographs of the cut ends, which I then compared, under my microscope, with the damaged telephone wires from Saxton Grange. The pattern of cuts made with the black handled knife was quite different to those on the severed ends of the telephone wire recovered from Saxton Grange, but the cuts made with the white handled knife were a perfect match.'

Out of the corner of his eye, Ernest could see that the jury looked suitably impressed, one or two of them nodding thoughtfully, as they passed around the album of photographs which had been prepared by the professor to demonstrate his point.

When Mr Streatfield got to his feet, he began with deceptive kindness. Would the professor care to tell the court how many other criminal trials in England had so far benefitted from his expertise in this particular matter?

Professor Tryhorn conceded that there had been no others so far, but hastened to add that he had previously performed numerous private experiments, involving this same technique.

'But none of these experiments have ever been accepted in a British court of law – when presented by you, or indeed by anyone else?'

'Not in this country, no.' The witness hesitated again, before adding. 'But I believe it has been done before in other countries.'

'Other countries.' Counsel for the defence managed to invest the words with the kind of contempt with which any decent Englishman would regard the customs of a head shrinking tribe in some distant jurisdiction, untrod by civilised man. 'And these photographs, professor, forgive me, but it is actually rather difficult to make out these matches between one pattern of cuts and another. The photographs are not particularly clear, are they?'

'Well, you see, if you will let me explain what they show…'

'They are, are they not, photographs of photographs, rather than the actual, original photographs?'

'The originals were much clearer.'

'Why then did you not bring these originals with you for the jury to look at?'

'I endeavoured to use the images which best illustrated the similarity.'

'I am looking at the images numbered four and five and it appears that in one case you have bent the original photograph before re-taking it, in order to make the pattern fit, rather than presenting the original image to the court.'

Ernest could see out of the corner of his eye that the jurymen's expressions of acceptance had been replaced by doubt, and that some of them were now gazing at the photographs with open puzzlement. It was like the story of the Emperor's New Clothes, he thought. Mr Paley Scott had encouraged them all to go along with the professor, talking as if any intelligent fellow would be able to see at once, the way those scratches all matched up, whereas Mr Streatfield had given them permission to doubt the man of science – to subject the pictures to proper scrutiny and decide whether or not the fuzzy images proved anything at all.

'Some sections of the original photographs have been cut out, have they not?' Streatfield continued to challenge the witness. 'And if you had not bent the original photograph, the two sets of marks would not have matched up, would they?'

'It is true that I displaced one portion of the image,' Tryhorn blustered. 'But you see, I had to allow for the knife bending away, as it cut through the wire. The marks made by the black handled knife were quite different.'

'I do not dispute it. But the fact that the black handled knife does not leave the same marks as the white handled knife, is hardly the same as being able to say that the white handled knife is the only knife in the universe which could have made those marks – marks which are supposedly much clearer in the photographs which unfortunately you have not brought along for the jury to see today – is it?'

The professor glanced sideways and licked his lips. Like Ernest, he could see the expressions on the faces of the jury. They had closed the book of photographs now and were all awaiting his answer.

'Let us make this as simple as possible,' Mr Streatfield hooked his thumbs into the sides of his gown. 'Are you prepared to rule out the possibility that there is some other knife, somewhere in the world, perhaps even within this county, capable of making those same marks when it cuts through a telephone wire?'

'Well it is a question of probabilities…'

'Is it possible that there is another knife in existence which could make those marks on the wire? Yes or no?'

'I cannot rule it out completely, no.'

And that's sent him off with his tail between his legs, Ernest thought.

Dr Sutherland was called to the witness box next. He was the police surgeon who had examined what was left of poor old Freddie's body after the fire and in so doing had discovered the shot gun pellets. Ernest recognised him from that awful Wednesday morning, when what was left of Fred had been lifted out of the ruined motor car, dumped onto a canvas stretcher, then covered by a tarpaulin and taken off to be examined in the barn. He kept his face as expressionless as possible, though he couldn't help recalling that but for this wretched bloke's thoroughness, the whole business might have been put down to a tragic accident and he wouldn't be sitting here now.

Dr Sutherland, perhaps mindful of the grieving widow and other family members, endeavoured to avoid going into too much gruesome detail, as he explained how he had found the shotgun pellets in and around what remained of Fred's heart, and the shotgun wadding in what remained of his chest.

'There can be no doubt whatsoever, Dr Sutherland, that the shot would have killed Frederick Morton?' asked Mr Paley Scott.

'None whatsoever.'

Though this unequivocal evidence was helpful to the prosecution case, Dr Sutherland was unable to provide much more in the ways of clues which would throw any light on how Freddie had met his death. Yes he agreed, it was probable that the muzzle of the gun had been held close to Mr Morton's chest, but obviously there were no tell-tale scorch marks to be seen, since the body had then been subjected to a much greater level of burning. No, he did not agree with P C Broadhead that the position in which the body had been found, with the torso lying across the front seats indicated that Mr Morton had been shot first and then dragged into the car before the fire was started. 'During the course of a fire, a body which is in a sitting position may well fall forwards, or sideways, or the fire's effect on objects around it may cause it to collapse into a quite different pose to that which it occupied when the fire started. In this case the legs had been almost completely destroyed and the body was therefore bound to have shifted somewhat.'

Paley Scott got no further when he attempted to discover whether Fred had already been dead by the time the fire started, whether there was any evidence that he had attempted to defend himself, or whether Dr Sutherland could tell how long he had been dead, or at what time he had last eaten or drunk anything.

'I am unable to assist you on this matter,' Sutherland repeated. 'Because the fire damaged the body to such an extent that all the evidence on these points was destroyed.'

Aye, Ernest thought grimly. All the evidence bar the worst possible bit of it.

When it was his turn to question the witness, Mr Streatfield, after a sip of his water, adopted a business like tone. 'Now Dr Sutherland, you have told us that it was mere chance that the section of the body containing evidence of this single shot had survived the fire?'

'That is correct.'

'Would I be right in saying that if there had been additional shots, which had entered other parts of Mr Morton's body – the parts which did not survive the fire so well – you would not have been able to find them?'

'Well clearly, if a body part had perished in its entirety, there would be nothing left to examine.'

'Precisely so. Which means that we cannot be certain that Mr Morton died as a result of only one shot, can we?'

Dr Sutherland, who knew very well on whose side he was supposed to be batting, looked doubtful. 'Had there been any more shots in close proximity to the heart, I believe that evidence of them would have survived.'

'With due respect, Dr Sutherland, that is not what I asked you. Let me put his more simply. Can you absolutely rule out the possibility that the man who shot Frederick Morton on 5 or 6 September this year, fired more than one shot at his victim?'

'I cannot absolutely rule that out, no.'

'Now when a person is shot like that at close range, it would be usual for some of his blood to spray out from the wound immediately, isn't that so?'

'Yes, it is.'

'So we have a situation where Mr Frederick Morton has arrived home in his motor car. Someone was lying in wait for him, and that person shot him dead – either as he was still sitting in his motor car, or immediately after he got out of it. This happened in the close confines of the garage, which means that the assailant must have been standing pretty close to Mr Morton at the time?'

'I never said that Mr Morton was shot whilst he was in the garage,' Dr Sutherland put in quickly.

'Indeed not. My understanding is that you are unable to state where Mr Morton was at the fatal moment: whether he was standing or sitting, inside the car or out of it, am I right?'

'That is correct, yes.'

'Let us assume for a moment that Mr Morton's assailant was awaiting him in the garage and shot him at close range. In those circumstances, would you expect some blood to be found, not only on the shot gun, but also on the assailant's clothes?'

'I should say that in those circumstances, if that was what occurred,' the doctor said cautiously, 'then it would be likely that some blood would get onto the assailant's clothing.'

'A considerable amount?'

'A fair amount.'

'Enough to be noticeable?'

'Enough to be noticeable – if the gun was fired at close range, as you suggest.'

'Thank you, Dr Sutherland. Now finally I want to ask you again about the likely time of death.'

'I have already said that I cannot possibly estimate a time of death from the available remains.' Dr Sutherland sounded almost irritated.

Mr Streatfield on the other hand now sounded immensely pleased with himself, as he said, 'Quite so, Dr Sutherland. So you can confirm that it is entirely possible that Frederick Morton was not shot during the night of Tuesday 5 September, either at or before eleven thirty, but could have been shot during the early hours of Wednesday 6 September, at half past midnight, or one o'clock, or two o'clock, or indeed at any point up until the garage was set alight in the early hours of the morning?'

'I cannot say anything as to what time the shot was fired,' said Dr Sutherland, sulkily.

'Thank you, Dr Sutherland. No further questions.'

Another doctor, Doctor Roche Lynch, came next. He was a 'well known expert', Ernest had learned. Apparently what this amounted to was that Dr Lynch was someone who appeared regularly in court, to give evidence against people who were accused of doing various things. He made a good living out of it, according to Mr Hyams.

Dr Roche Lynch told the court that he had been provided with a shotgun taken from Saxton Grange and various items of clothing which had been taken from the prisoner following his arrest. The pile of folded clothing which had been lying on the central table alongside the motley collection of other objects, was offered for his inspection and he agreed that it represented the clothing which he had received for testing. He had thoroughly examined all these items for blood stains, he explained. He had found four spots of blood on the muzzle of the shotgun, but he was unable to say whose blood it was, or how it might have got there. As for Ernest's clothes, the only blood he had found was a tiny amount on the toe cap of one boot. It was definitely human blood, but he could not say to whom it belonged. Finally there was a smear of blood on the lower left leg of Ernest's trousers, but it was so small that there was insufficient to test whether it was human blood or not.

'Well then that represents absolutely nothing,' harrumphed the judge, whose patience had already been tried by the professor from Hull.

'With respect, my lord, I think it has come from the trouser rubbing against the boot and is therefore likely to be human blood,' the expert witness ventured.

'Pah. It might have come from a rabbit, or anything. Any countryman may have a trace of blood on him from a whole variety of causes.' Travers Humphreys was becoming more and more irritated with Dr Lynch.

He can see that this Lynch is a crafty little weasel, Ernest thought. More interested in earning his fee by helping the prosecution, than he is in really getting at the truth. Paid experts. It was dirty money so far as he could see, with the whole charabanc load of them tailoring their evidence in the hopes of getting a man hanged.

Ernest could sense that the old biddies were getting restless too. They were probably bored by all this technical stuff, experiments with microscopes and chemical tests. It was a complete anti-climax after the intimations of flirtation and adultery, which had come the day before. There was no titillation to be had in fragments of cut up wire or arguments about shot gun cartridges.

At least the next witness presented a familiar face. Ernest watched as his old mate, Wally Wright, entered the court room and walked across to the witness box. Wally was appearing for the prosecution, but that did not stop him being a friend, and unlike so many of the ordinary witnesses, Wally did not seem overawed by his surroundings. Perhaps being a pub landlord had invested him with a little more confidence than the likes of Murray Stuart. Or maybe it was because Wally had no axe to grind and intended to tell it straight.

As usual, Mr Paley Scott went first, guiding Wally through what had happened on the day of 5 September. Yes, Wally agreed, Ernest had arrived at his pub, the Malt Shovel in Tadcaster, at around midday or probably just after, and asked Wally if he fancied joining him on a run out to Greetland in the horse box: an offer to which Wally had readily agreed. They had stopped at the Junction Inn at Heckmondwike for a bite of lunch, then gone on to the farm at Greetland, where Ernest had made his abortive attempt to deliver Mr Morton's cow. There had been a bit of a hold up there, Wally said, and then they had driven home, stopping for a couple of pints at another hostelry along the way and finally getting back to the Malt Shovel, at between eight o'clock to a quarter past eight.

'And here Brown dropped you off?'

'That's right.'

'Did he get down from the lorry and come into the inn?'

'No, he stayed in the cab and once I'd got down, he said he'd see me later and drove straight back in the direction of Saxton Grange.'

None of Wally Wright's evidence was a source of dispute and Mr Streatfield contented himself with just a couple of questions.

'As someone who knew Ernest Brown well, Mr Wright, how would you describe his mood that day?'

'He was in good spirits, laughing and joking like.'

'Right up until he left you at the Malt Shovel?'

'Yes.'

'You mentioned that when he dropped you back at the inn, he said that he would see you later. Is it the case, Mr Wright, that Ernest Brown had arranged to come back, in order to give a lift to a friend of your wife's, later that evening?'

'Yes. Mrs Littlewood, a friend of my wife's, had come to visit and Ernest – that is Mr Brown – had promised to give her a lift into Leeds, later that evening, so that she could catch a bus from there, back to her home.'

'So you definitely expected the defendant, Ernest Brown, to return to your inn, later that same evening?'

'Yes, sir. That is correct.'

'But Ernest Brown did not come back?'

'No sir. Ernest did not come back.'

After Wally it was the turn of Annie Littlewood to enter the witness box and take the oath. Was she a friend of Mrs Wright, Mr Paley Scott wanted to know.

'I am. And of Mr Wright too.'

'Quite so. Now tell me Mrs Littlewood, were you visiting Mrs Wright at the Malt Shovel public house in Tadcaster on 5 September?'

'I was.'

'You live at some distance from there I believe?'

'I do. I live at Heckmondwike.'

'Had you made any arrangements for getting back home from the Malt Shovel that evening?'

'I had.' Mrs Littlewood pursed her lips, as if these thwarted arrangements still rankled with her in some way.

'Can you kindly tell the court how you had planned to get home that evening?'

'It had been arranged earlier in the day that Mr Brown would give me a lift into Leeds, where I could get a bus back to Heckmondwike.'

'The jury may not be familiar with the transport arrangements in that part of the East Riding, Mrs Littlewood, so perhaps you could explain the significance of obtaining a lift into Leeds.'

Mrs Littlewood nodded, turning her attention more directly to the jury before she spoke. 'There's no direct bus from Tadcaster to Heckmondwike, so you have to change in Leeds, but the last bus from Tadcaster to Leeds leaves at about half six. If you can get a lift into Leeds after that bus has gone, it means that you can stay longer in Tadcaster and get a much later bus back to Heckmondwike.'

'So it had definitely been arranged that the man in the dock, Ernest Brown, would drive you into Leeds to catch this later bus?'

'That's right.'

'But that did not occur, did it? Will you kindly tell the court what actually happened?'

'Well, I had my tea with Mrs Wright and then Mr Wright was dropped off at the front door, and he came inside and said that Ernest Brown would be back within half an hour or so with his boss's motor car, and would run me into Leeds, only time went on and on and he never turned up.' Mrs Littlewood paused, glancing somewhat resentfully towards the man in the dock, then back to Mr Paley Scott, who nodded encouragingly. 'We were starting to get a bit vexed like,' she continued. 'Wally – that is Mr Wright – said that it was cutting it a bit fine and not like Ernest to let folk down. We thought that maybe something had happened up at the farm, with one of the horses or something, but of course there would have been no way of him letting us know that, because there's no telephone at the Malt Shovel. Anyway Mr Wright has the telephone number of Saxton Grange, so he wrote it on a piece of paper for me and I went to the telephone booth in the Market Place – Mr Wright would have gone himself, only he had customers and couldn't leave the bar – and I got through to the telephone exchange and asked for the number on the paper, but there was no reply.'

'And this was at what time, Mrs Littlewood?' interposed the judge.

'At about ten o'clock, sir.'

'This would be the much later call already referred to by the telephone operator, Miss Morris of the Tadcaster exchange, my lord,' said the ever-helpful Paley Scott.

'Thank you, Mr Paley Scott.' Travers Humphreys nodded gravely. 'Please continue, Mrs Littlewood.'

She regarded him doubtfully. 'I'm not sure that there is anything else to say, my lord.'

'Perhaps you could tell the court how in fact you did get home,' suggested Mr Paley Scott.

'Well, I didn't. Not that night. Mr and Mrs Wright had to make up a bed for me, in their spare room and then I got the bus home the next morning.'

'Thank you, Mrs Littlewood, I have no further questions.'

'I have no questions for this witness, my lord,' said Mr Streatfield.

Mrs Littlewood was allowed to stand down and her place was taken by yet another familiar face who was also the keeper of licensed premises – in this case the Old George Hotel, at Garforth Bridge. As Maria Jackson took the stand, she stole a look at Ernest and he nodded in acknowledgement, as politely as if they'd seen one another across a crowded street. She had a nervous look about her, he noted, and was clearly not sure whether she ought to crack a smile at him or not. A woman anxious to do the right thing, trying to give of her best in a difficult set of circumstances.

'Yes,' Mrs Jackson agreed, in answer to the initial questions from Mr Paley Scott, she had known the late Frederick Morton fairly well and Ernest Brown too. They had both been regular customers at her pub.

'Did you see either of these men on Tuesday 5 September?' asked Mr Paley Scott,

Ernest had already fallen into the rhythm of the procedure for extracting information, but he observed that Maria Jackson appeared momentarily puzzled at being asked a question by someone who knew the answer perfectly well already. So she hesitated, and then as if falling in with the rules of some new game, replied, 'Yes, I saw Mr Morton. He called in twice that day.'

'And at what time did these visits take place?'

'The first time it was at about one o'clock in the afternoon, though I can't place the time exactly, and then he came in again at about quarter to six.'

'How long was Mr Morton there on each occasion?'

'Well, when he came in at lunch time it was just for a quick pint. He was in and out, so to speak. He was there a bit longer in the evening. He had two glasses of my best bitter, while he was stood at the bar, talking.'

'Was he talking with you?'

'He was. There were no other customers standing at the bar just then.'

'Can you remember what the two of you talked about?'

Mrs Jackson paused, as if considering. 'It was just an ordinary chat, not about anything in particular.'

'And how did Mr Morton seem to you? Did he seem worried, concerned, upset in any way?'

'Mr Morton was just his usual self. He was perfectly happy.'

'And what time did he leave?'

'It was seven o'clock, give or take five minutes.'

'Was he sober?'

'As a judge. Oops sorry, my lord.' Mrs Jackson recovered herself quickly. 'He was perfectly sober.'

'Did he say where he was going?'

'He said he was going home.'

'Thank you, Mrs Jackson. No further questions.'

Mr Streatfield favoured the witness with a smile. 'Tell me, Mrs Jackson. Have you often seen Mr Morton and the defendant, Ernest Brown drinking together, in your pub?'

'Oh yes. Often.'

'How did they seem to you?'

'Like good friends.'

'How did Ernest Brown behave towards Mr Morton?'

'Well, they were always friendly. Mr Brown was respectful of course and always treated Mr Morton like you would an employer, but it was very friendly on both sides.'

'You never saw any antagonism, or quarrelling?'

'No. None whatsoever.'

The final prosecution witness was Frank Cawood, another ruddy faced countryman, who looked ill at ease in his stiff collar and a dark suit bought for a funeral which had been held when he was several pounds lighter. He had even put on his old Dad's watch and chain, Ernest noticed, probably in order to invest himself with a degree of formality, appropriate to this unaccustomed environment.

'You are a farmer, are you not?' began Mr Paley Scott, whose friendly overtures seemed lost on Cawood, who was clearly nervous and merely nodded vigorously in response, until firmly reminded that he had to answer all the questions out loud.

'Aye, yes I am. That's right.' Having found his tongue, Cawood now appeared desirous of answering the question three times over, thereby provoking some stifled mirth in the public gallery.

'Your mother is the licensee of a public house, known as the Boot and Shoe, at Peckfield, is she not?'

'That's correct.'

'One moment if you please, Mr Paley Scott.' The judge spoke in the same irritable tone which he had adopted when reference had previously been made to plans of the farm. 'Is this place, Peckfield, marked on the map that has been provided as an exhibit?'

'It is my lord.'

'For the benefit of the jury, can you please confirm for us, how far these various hostelries are from the scene of the crime?'

'Of course, my lord.' Paley Scott referred to his notes. 'Peckfield is between five and six miles from Saxton Grange.'

'And it would take approximately how long to travel between one and the other in a motor car?'

'The police undertook to time it, my lord and they say that it takes no more than ten minutes and can of course be done in rather less.'

'And from the hotel belonging to the last witness?'

'It is seven miles from Mrs Jackson's inn at Garforth Bridge to Saxton Grange, my lord.'

'And between Garforth Bridge and Peckfield?'

'Less than a mile, my lord. No more than four or five minutes' drive at most.'

'Thank you, Mr Paley Scot. Please proceed.'

'Thank you my lord.' Turning back to the witness, the barrister resumed: 'On Tuesday 5 September, you were at the Boot and Shoe, helping your mother behind the bar were you not?'

'Aye, I was. The feller what normally helps out was off with a bad foot, so she was shorthanded.'

'And during the course of the evening, Mr Frederick Morton came in and ordered a drink?'

'He did.'

'You knew him well.'

'Very well indeed.'

'Was he alone?'

'He was.'

'How did he seem to you?'

Cawood appeared to consider a moment. 'His usual self.'

'Was he drunk?'

'No.'

'Did he seem unhappy in any way?'

'No.'

'Worried?'

'No.'

'Did you have a conversation with him?'

'I did.'

'What about?'

'I sold him some cattle cake. He bargained with me for a while, and beat me down in price.'

He would do, Ernest thought.

'But it was a good humoured exchange?'

'Perfectly,' Cawood agreed. 'We'd done business plenty of times before.'

'At what time did Mr Morton arrive and leave that evening?'

'As far as I can recall, he came in at about quarter past eight and he left half an hour later.'

'Did he say where he was going next?'

'No.'

When it was Mr Streatfield's turn, he wanted to know how much Freddie Morton had drunk while he was at the Boot and Shoe.

'He had two glasses of bitter.'

'I see you are wearing a very handsome watch and chain, Mr Cawood. Were you wearing it on 5 September?'

'No.'

'How then do you fix the time that Mr Morton arrived and left that evening?'

Cawood gaped, his big bullock's eyes widening. 'I don't rightly know.'

'You didn't look at your watch. In fact you have told the court that you were not wearing it. Did you particularly look at, or comment on the time, when Mr Morton arrived, or left?'

'No. I had no reason for fixing the time.' Cawood sounded disgruntled.

'So it is just an estimate?'

'Aye, just an estimate.'

'Thank you, Mr Cawood. That is all.'

CHAPTER TEN

Thursday 14 December 1933
Leeds Town Hall, The Yorkshire Assizes

As he took the oath, his hand on the New Testament, Ernest squared his shoulders and reminded himself that he was as good a man as any one of them, for all their educated words, their pomp and ceremony. Yet in spite of his determination, his throat dried and his words rasped out of it like leaves blown along the lane on an autumn afternoon.

As Mr Streatfield stood up and approached him, everything else seemed to loom closer as well. After watching from the slight elevation of the dock, Ernest now found himself hemmed in by hostility, with the judge above him to the right, the public gallery rising higher still to his left, the journalists at his back and the jury staring straight into his face. Only Mr Streatfield, on his feet and approaching to start his questions, presented a countenance which could have been described as remotely friendly.

'Ernest Brown, can you please tell the court how long you had been working for Frederick Morton, by September of this year?'

He tried to speak but the words would not come. His answer emerged as little more than a whisper.

'Speak up, please.' For once that fussy old devil on the platform sounded almost friendly. 'This is your opportunity to tell your side of the story, you know. It is no use if we cannot hear you.'

Ernest nodded, took encouragement and said firmly, 'Yes, my lord,' before he began again. This time he remembered to breathe in the right places, to look Mr Streatfield straight in the eye. Ignore the old biddies, ignore the jury, and ignore the bloody judge too, unless directly spoken to. Tell his side of the story. Yes, right.

They had already agreed, in one of those conversations which had taken place in the little, tiled cell, in the basement of the building, that Mr Streatfield would ask him very little about the affair with Dolly, except to establish whether he had ever been violent toward her, or threatened her in any way – questions to which Ernest responded with firm denials.

'Were you ever jealous, when she paid attention to other men?'

'No.'

'Did you make threats toward her or anyone else, in order to regain your job in June?'

'No.'

'And after you returned to work at Saxton Grange in June, did you continue to be intimate with Mrs Morton?'

'No.'

'Were you unhappy about that?'

'No.'

'So you had no wish to coerce her into continuing this relationship of intimacy which you had formerly enjoyed?'

'No.' He repeated the word again and again, calmly, but firmly. With each response, he was conscious that his voice had strengthened and was carrying greater conviction.

'How long had you known Mr Frederick Morton Jnr.?'

'I should say about sixteen or seventeen years, certainly since he was still in school.'

'And did you get along well with him?'

'I liked Mr Morton and we were rather good friends, though I did not always like the way he did business, or treated his customers.'

'Did you ever have disagreements with him?'

'We occasionally disagreed over the price he had paid for horses, but that was purely business. It didn't affect our friendship.'

'Did you ever make threats against Mr Morton? For example saying that you would like to hit him?'

'I don't remember making threats about hitting him, but I may have done. If so, then I did not mean it. I may have said it as a joke.'

'So it was never your intention to hit Mr Morton.'

'If it had been my intention, then I would have carried it out.'

'Did you ever threaten to wreck Mr Morton's business?'

'I did not. I did once say that we would all be out of work in a couple of months, if things went on as they were.'

'And what made you say that?'

'Because we were doing very little trade at the time and Mr Morton had been saying earlier that day, that we would have to have a round-up of all the cattle, where the customers were behind with their instalments.'

'Do you remember saying that the business would run better without Mr Morton?'

'No – and if I ever did, then it would only have been in jest.'

'Now after you had returned to work for Mr Morton in June, you were allocated a different set of duties, were you not? Can you tell the court about your new job?'

'I was to drive the new horse box, take charge of maintaining the family's motor cars, and the tractors used on the farm, and I was also to try out all the heavy horses that were bought.'

'Were you unhappy with these new responsibilities?'

'No I preferred them. Mr Morton had already been planning to move the jobs around before I left and was in the process of taking on a new groom in place of me. He was only waiting on the new horse box being delivered before he put the new arrangements in place.'

'Why did you prefer the new arrangements?'

'There was less heavy work and mucking out, and being put in charge of the horse box got me out and about, driving around the countryside, which I enjoyed.'

'And there was no reduction in your wages?'

'No. I was paid exactly the same as before.'

'Did you consider that fair?'

'Perfectly fair.'

Though Fred had driven a hard bargain with his suppliers and customers, he had always been fair with his own men, Ernest thought. Two pounds ten shillings a week and all found, had been ample enough to tempt a man who was good with stock, such as himself, to work out in the sticks. As for driving the horse box, it was no more than the truth that he had loved to get out in the country, bowling along between the hedgerows that summer – in fact he could remember days when he had sung for the sheer joy of it. How often had he thanked his lucky stars that unlike most of the men, he had learned to drive and thereby earned for himself a role in the business which had given him the freedom of the open road?

Now that he thought about it, he fancied that he and Wally had sung a few choruses of 'Tipperary', that very day in September, as they had driven back from the errand in Greetland, with the shadows of the late summer afternoon lengthening. The day to which Mr Streatfield was now recalling his attention. The day when everything had been about to go all wrong.

'I want you to cast your mind back to Tuesday 5 September,' Mr Streatfield was saying. 'Can you tell us what kind of morning that was?'

Ernest hesitated. Did he mean to ask about the weather, or what? 'It was an ordinary morning,' he said.

'Just another ordinary day on the farm?'

'Yes.' Up at half past six as usual. Chores to do. Horses calling for their breakfast, their heads appearing out of loose boxes at the approach of boots across the yard. Buckets clanking as they were carried across from the trough, greetings called out, as one by one the other men arrived for work, the familiar sounds soon topped off by the distinctive clang of the blacksmith's hammer.

'At some point in the day, were you asked to take the horsebox out?'

'Yes. At about midday, Mr Morton told me to load up a cow and take her to Harry Lumb's farm, at Greetland.'

'And what did you do, in response to this?'

'I loaded the cow and left at about quarter past twelve.'

'Did you stop in Tadcaster to pick up Mr Wright?'

'I did.'

'Do you think Mr Morton would have had any objection to that arrangement?'

'I knew that he would not. I wouldn't have taken Mr Wright along with me, if I had thought that Mr Morton would object.'

'What happened when you reached Mr Lumb's farm?'

'After I had unloaded the cow and he had looked her over, he said that the beast was not what he wanted and that I was to take her back.'

'So you put the cow back into the horsebox and drove back to Saxton Grange. Now, on your way, you stopped at Tadcaster, did you not, to drop your friend Mr Wright, back at the Malt Shovel?'

'I did.'

'And you told him that you would see him again later?'

'Yes, after I had taken the cow back and done my other chores.'

'At what time did you leave the Malt Shovel?'

'It was between eight o'clock and a quarter past.'

'Very well. Now please tell us what happened next.'

'I drove back to the farm. It would take me about ten minutes.' Almost exactly ten minutes. He knew the road like the back of his hand. Knew the very moment when the roof of the farmhouse came into view. Knew the sound of the gravel under the tyres as he turned the big vehicle in through the always-open gates at the top of the drive, passing the Essex, which had been left as it often was, pulled in to the side, leaving only just enough room for him to get the lorry by. The tight left hand turn into the yard at the back of the farmhouse, still bright with its new paint: white stonework, with the woodwork all picked out in blue, the colours of Fred's football team, Huddersfield Town. They were both Huddersfield men. It was part of the bond between them. And as he drove down into the yard, there at the water trough had been the familiar figure of Dolly herself, filling buckets for the horses.

'Did you see anyone when you reached Saxton Grange? Can you tell us what happened when you arrived there?'

'When I drove into the yard, I noticed Mrs Morton was filling buckets, at the water trough. I turned off the engine, got down from the cab, then went straight round the back and started taking down the ramp, ready to unload the cow. Mrs Morton came over to help me. I asked her where the boss was, and told her that I wanted to go back out again, shortly.'

'And what did she say?'

'She said, "Oh do you?"'

'Did you ask her what she had been doing that afternoon?'

'No, I didn't, but she told me that she had been swimming at Wetherby.'

'She simply volunteered this information without being asked?'

'That's right.'

'Were you in any way upset by this?'

'No. I was not particularly interested.'

'Have you any idea why she told you about going swimming with another man, that afternoon?'

'You would be better asking her.'

Mr Streatfield's eyes conveyed a warning look. There was nothing to be gained, from getting too cheeky.

'Did you, at any point, drag Mrs Morton across the yard?'

'No.'

'Did you push her over?'

'I did not.'

'Can you tell us what you did do?'

'I had a halter on the cow and Mrs Morton helped me to walk her into the mistal and as we were both coming out again, Mrs Morton got in my way and I pushed her. It was accidental, but the floor was greasy and she slipped and fell.'

'Did you assist her to her feet?'

'No. She got up before I could help her. She was annoyed, and she said, "You have done something that you will be sorry for."'

'And what did you reply?'

'I think I said something in apology, but she was still angry. Then I went into the barn to fetch some hay for the cow and I think she followed me in there. I heard her calling out something, but I'm not sure what she said, because I was up the ladder in the loft by then. While I was still up there I heard another voice outside in the yard, which must have been Miss Houseman, and after that it went quiet and I assumed that they must have both gone inside.'

'So what did you do next?'

'I got on with my chores. I took the horsebox round to the muck heap and part cleared it out. I only part did the job as I wanted to get done in time to catch the bus that passes the road end at nine o'clock. I intended to finish the job off the next morning.'

'You intended to catch the bus back to Tadcaster?'

'Yes.'

'Had you not made an arrangement to take the Essex car and give Mrs Littlewood a lift into Leeds?'

'No. There was no firm arrangement made with Mrs Littlewood. I never used the car without the master's permission, and as he was not there to give it, I intended to catch the bus.' It made him feel uncomfortable, to contradict Wally's evidence in this way, but there was no helping it.

'So,' Mr Streatfield prompted. 'After you had dealt with the horsebox, then what did you do?'

'I went into the house. Miss Houseman was in the kitchen and I asked her to fetch Mrs Morton, so that I could speak with her. I waited while she fetched Mrs

Morton and then I explained to her about the cow – so that she could tell Mr Morton when he came home. Then I asked her for some help getting the ducks in for the night.'

'Was this a usual thing?'

'Oh yes. It's much easier to do with two of you, and Mrs Morton had often helped in the past, but that night she said she couldn't, as she was waiting for a phone call from her father.'

'Had she ever refused to help with the ducks before?'

'Never.' He could not resist glancing in Dolly's direction, but she was staring straight ahead, as if fascinated by the coat of arms above the judge's chair.

'Could you not have asked Miss Houseman to help you?'

'Miss Houseman never helped with that kind of job and anyway she was making jam, which I think has to be stirred all the time and can't be left.'

'So you went outside and rounded up the ducks by yourself. Roughly what time was it when you were dealing with the ducks?'

'By the time I'd got the ducks in, it would have been just past nine. I was too late for the bus by then, so I carried on with a few more jobs. While I was working around the yard, I saw some rats running about, so I went inside, got the gun and had a couple of shots at one of them.'

'So, you had been outside pretty much continuously between half past eight and half past nine, which is when you shot at the rats. During that time, if a car had arrived, would you have seen or heard it?'

'Most certainly.'

'Would any car which arrived have been audible to anyone sitting in the kitchen?'

'Definitely. You can always hear a car coming down the drive, wherever you are in the yard or in the house.'

'I would like you to tell me a little more about the whereabouts of the shotgun while it was in your possession that evening. Did you for example, take the gun down the drive to the garage at any point?'

'No. I never took the gun any further than the yard. When I first got it out, I propped it up near the kitchen door, while I waited for the rats to reappear. When I saw one, I took a first shot at it in the yard, but I missed it, so I followed it into the mistal and took a second shot at it there, but I still didn't manage to hit it. After that I propped the gun up alongside the kitchen door again for a little while, until I'd finished what I was doing and was ready to take it inside. Later on, I took it into the kitchen, where I cleaned it and put it away.'

'And what were you doing, between shooting at the rat and taking the gun inside?'

'After I shot at the rat, I heard a horse loose somewhere. I went to find it and saw that it had broken its head collar. That wasn't an unusual thing with that particular animal. I looked for a spare head collar in the stables, but I couldn't find a suitable one, so I went up to the attic, where the rest of the spare ropes and collars are kept. I found a leather head collar up there and a rope shank. I took them downstairs and fastened the horse with them. It was getting dark by then and I'd got no light in the stable, so I struck a match to see what I was doing and this startled the horse. It flew back and in doing so, it pulled tight the chowl band – that's the bit that goes under its jaw. I couldn't undo it and had to go into the house to get a knife to cut it free.'

'Can you remember what knife you fetched from the house that night?'

'I fetched the black handled knife. I'd been using it for odd jobs ever since I mislaid my own pocket knife, a few weeks before. As I cut the chowl band free, I nicked my thumb – it bled a little bit, but not very much.'

'While you had this knife outside the house, did you cut the telephone wires?' The barrister made it sound like a completely innocuous question. He might have been enquiring about the time of the next bus.

'No, I did not.' He delivered his response in a similarly deadpan tone.

'Do you recall any conversation with Mrs Morton around this time, regarding a telephone call?'

'When I was either fetching the knife or putting it back – I can't remember which – Mrs Morton said something about there having been a phone call from Scotland, and I said, "Oh, has there?"'

'Had you heard the telephone bell yourself?'

'No.'

'So you were surprised when Mrs Morton mentioned that there had been a call?'

'Not particularly. I can't say that I took much notice. It hadn't really got anything to do with me.'

'When you came down from the attic, carrying the rope and the head collar, did you notice that Mrs Morton and Miss Houseman appeared to be afraid of you?'

'I can't say that I did.'

'Can you think of any reason why the women might have been afraid of you that evening?'

'No.'

'When you brought the gun back into the kitchen, did you use it to threaten or intimidate them in any way?'

'No. I had no reason to threaten them.'

'Do you have any idea why Miss Houseman was afraid to take the gun from you, when she was offered it?'

'None whatever.'

'And after you had cleaned the gun and put it away, what did you do then?'

'I went outside and put the Essex car away. I coasted it down the drive, because when I tried to start it, I found that the battery was flat. After that I went back to my hut and changed my boots for my slippers. Then I loosed the Great Dane from her kennel and she followed me back into the kitchen. Miss Houseman was still waiting for the jam to be done and Mrs Morton was doing her sewing. The three of us sat talking for quite a while, just about ordinary things, the horses and the farm and such like, and eventually I went out again to the wash house. It was about half past eleven by then and while I was outside, I heard the boss's car coming in. He pulled up on the drive, just above the garage, and I went down to meet him and told him about bringing back the cow from Greetland.'

'Was he alone?'

'Yes.'

'Did he get out of the car?'

'No, we spoke through the open window. I told him about the cow, and he said "Oh bugger, another wasted journey," or words to that effect.'

'And how did Mr Morton appear to you?'

'He was very much the worse for drink. His speech was slurred. I asked him if he wanted me to put the car away for him and he said, "no," as he might be going out again.'

'What did you do then?'

'I left him to it. I could hear him shunting the car back and forth and racing the engine.'

'Did you see or hear him go back out again?'

'No.'

'And then what happened?'

'I went back into the house and told Mrs Morton about the conversation I'd just had with her husband. After that I sat in the kitchen for about another quarter of an hour, then I went outside again to put the dog in its kennel and stoked up the boiler for the night. When I went back into the kitchen the next time, neither of the women was there, so I guessed that they'd gone up to bed.'

'Were there any lights burning in the house at this point?'

'Only the lamp in the kitchen. That's always left burning all night.'

'What did you do when you went back into the house on this occasion?'

'I had a wash at the kitchen sink, then I had a glass of milk and a slice of bread and butter. I hadn't eaten my supper that night on account of it being cold sausages, which I don't like. After that I took off my shirt collar and my tie, which I always leave in my jacket pocket, ready for me to slip them straight back on again. I'd already left my jacket hanging over the back of the kitchen chair, which I always do in the summer months, and then I went out to my hut, where I went straight to bed. I didn't wear my pyjamas, on account of it being a hot night. I went off to sleep pretty much straight away and I didn't see or hear anything else until after the fire had started.' He was tempted to glance across at the jury, in order to see what they were making of this radically different interpretation of the evening's events, but then he recalled Mr Streatfield's advice and stayed focussed on his barrister instead.

'It was by no means the first time that Mr Morton had arrived home, somewhat the worse for drink, was it?'

'It was not the first time, no.'

'Had Mr Morton sometimes fallen asleep in his car and spent the night in the garage?'

'Several times.'

'Is that what you thought had happened on this occasion?'

'I didn't know what had happened. It was none of my affair.'

'So after you had gone off to sleep, what was the next thing you heard?'

'I was awoken by an explosion – at least it sounded like an explosion.'

'Was it like a gunshot?'

'No. More of a dull thud. I sat up in bed and I could see the glow of the fire through the window. I got up and went outside to see what was going on, and from there I could see that the garage was on fire. I quickly pulled on my shirt, trousers, waistcoat and slippers – because they went on quicker than my boots – and then I ran straight round to the garage, but I couldn't get near for the heat of the flames, so I ran back up to the house, intending to rouse the household. I was calling out Mrs Morton's name, but then I realised that they were already up, so I got all the beasts out of the adjacent buildings, started up the horsebox and moved that out of harm's way, and after that I ran back to the house.'

As he spoke he could still remember the heat from the flames, the filthy smells as everything from tins of paint to human flesh were consumed by the voracious blaze. He heard again the panic stricken calls of the beasts in the stables, their fear soon mirrored by his own, as the fire began to spread across the rafters and waves of acrid smoke found their way in through the porous walls and open windows. He remembered how Inkerman, the big black stallion had reared up and all but crushed him, as he tried to get the creature out to safety. He had got every last one of them out, he thought, hampered by a cloak of darkness which was alleviated only by the unearthly light of the fire itself, and with every moment that passed there had been the possibility that he might become trapped by the flames or succumb to the smoke. He ought to have got a ruddy medal, but instead he had ended up on trial here, with his life in the balance again.

'And when you reached the house?' prompted Mr Streatfield.

'There was no sign of Mrs Morton, so I went into the drawing room and tried the telephone. I thought there might be something wrong with it, because the receiver was already lying off the hook when I got there, but I still tried dialling 01 for the exchange. When no one answered I decided that as I couldn't get a reply on the telephone, I would be best getting help in the village, so I grabbed my jacket, got into the horse box and drove into Towton, where I woke Mr Stuart, and while I was there, either him or me got someone to ring for the fire brigade.'

'What else did you do, while you were waiting for Mr Stuart?'

'I put on my collar and tie and ran a hand over my hair. It always stays pretty flat anyway, on account of the hair oil I use.'

'So then you drove Mr Stuart back to the farm,' Streatfield prompted.

'I did, but there wasn't much we could do on our own. Mr Stuart said that he thought the boss might be in the garage and I agreed that he could be. As the womenfolk were nowhere to be seen, we decided to go for the police. I drove the horsebox, as Stuart cannot drive.' (And that had been another source of jealousy, Ernest thought.) 'We went to PC Broadhead's cottage and he followed us back to the farm on his bicycle. By the time we got back to Saxton Grange, Mrs Morton had already been brought back from the village in somebody's car. She was standing on the drive, looking at the fire and when she saw me, she told me to start playing the hose onto the loose boxes, to stop the fire from spreading to them, which I did.'

'Did you say anything at all to Mrs Morton about a rope, at this time?'

'No.'

'Did you threaten to hang her, using a rope left on the landing?'

'No. I did not threaten to hang her with a rope. I did not threaten her with anything. PC Broadhead was standing only a few yards away from us the whole time and in any case I had no reason to threaten her.' He wondered what the jury would make of the obvious exasperation in his tone.

Mr Streatfield's expression appeared to offer both caution and encouragement. In a slightly louder voice than he had used hitherto, the defending barrister commenced on his final salvo of questions.

'Did you kill Mr Morton?'

'No.'

'Did you shoot at Mr Morton with that gun?'

'No, sir.'

'Did you set fire to the garage?'

'No, sir.'

'Did you set fire to the cars, or to anything else in the garage?'

'No, sir.'

'Did you cut the telephone wires?'

'No.'

'Have you any knowledge at all, of how Mr Morton met his death?'

'I have not – not in the slightest.'

A moment of silence lay across the court room, sharp and cold as the frost which would settle across the fields of Saxton Grange that night, before darkness had turned to dawn.

CHAPTER ELEVEN

Thursday 14 December 1933
Leeds Town Hall, The Yorkshire Assizes

The flicker of what might almost have been a smile passed briefly across the countenance of Mr Paley Scott, as he rose to cross-examine the man in the witness box. Now I have you, his expression seemed to say. This is the opportunity that I have been waiting for. The moment to carve up your testimony, piece by piece, and throw it to the dogs.

Ernest faced him unflinching, looking him right in the eye, just as he had Mr Streatfield.

'Tell me, Mr Brown,' the prosecution barrister adopted an unexpectedly friendly tone. 'How did you address the late Mr Morton? Did you say, "Mr Morton"? Or was it "Boss"?'

'I used to call him Fred.'

'I see – that's nice and short, isn't it? Much quicker to say "Fred" than to say "Mrs Morton", wouldn't you agree?'

'Yes, I would.'

'So when you found the garage was on fire and you tried to raise the household, why did you shout out "Mrs Morton", when you could far more easily have shouted "Fred"?'

'I knew Mrs Morton was at home. I did not know whether Mr Morton had eventually come home or not.'

'But surely you did not really expect that Mr Morton would have spent the whole night in the garage?'

'He'd done so before.'

Mr Paley Scott abruptly switched tack. 'Today you have told this court that you attempted to call for the fire brigade, using the drawing room telephone. Why did you not mention this to PC Broadhead on the morning of the fire?'

'He didn't ask me anything about the telephone.'

'But you did not volunteer the information.'

'He asked me two or three questions about waking up and finding the garage on fire and he took the answers down in his notebook. He never asked anything about the telephone, or even who had sent for the fire brigade. I was not suspected of setting the fire, nor yet charged with murder, then.'

Mr Paley Scott had reached for and was consulting a sheet of paper, from the pile on his table. 'Here in the statement which you gave to Superintendent Blacker, it says that you did not think of calling for the fire brigade.'

'Superintendent Blacker asked me a series of questions and then he wrote down my answers. He asked me why I had not *immediately* tried to telephone for the fire brigade and I said that I didn't think of it, because what I thought about first was the horses screaming in their boxes, and the need to get them out of the way of the fire, which is naturally what anybody would do in that situation.'

'But surely you would have then mentioned to Superintendent Blacker, that you had subsequently tried to use the telephone and received no reply?'

'After I had given him my answer to that question, he asked me another one which had nothing at all to do with the telephone.'

'So you did not think of attempting to get help by using the telephone until the garage was well alight, and then it somehow slipped your mind until much later that you had ever tried to do so at all?'

'No,' said Ernest firmly. 'It never slipped my mind at all. It only comes across that way, because that's the way Superintendent Blacker put the question. As for saving the horses first, if you had been in my place, woken up in the early hours of the morning, with the buildings already well ablaze and the animals trapped and terrified, you'd have done the same.'

'When you tried the telephone, did you not think it very strange that you couldn't get any answer?'

'Not particularly. I'd never tried to make a call so late and I wasn't sure if the exchange worked all night… Besides which, the telephone at Saxton Grange was always going wrong.'

'Did you know there was another telephone in the office?'

'Of course.'

'And though the office had been locked up for the night, you knew where the keys were kept did you not? Did it not occur to you to try calling from the office?'

'I knew where the keys were, but I thought that if the one telephone was out of order then the other one would be as well.'

'You did not realise that the telephone in the office would still connect to the exchange, even though the wire to the house telephone had been cut?'

'I didn't know that any wires had been cut. Usually when the one telephone doesn't work, you find the other one isn't working either.'

'Have you ever known Mr Morton to come in at half past eleven at night and go straight out again?'

'Not so far as I can remember.'

'So you must have thought it strange for Mr Morton to suggest such a thing?'

'I didn't think anything about it at all. It was nothing to do with me.'

'He was not in a fit condition to be driving a motor car, was he?'

'That was why I offered to put it in the garage for him, but he declined.'

'Surely, if you were such a good friend to Mr Morton as you now say that you were,' Mr Paley Scott's question slid snake-like towards the witness box, ready to ensnare him, 'then it was your duty to prevent him from leaving the premises again in such a state?'

'I was not in a position to prevent Mr Morton from doing anything. That would have been far in excess of my duties.'

'But surely, if you had prevented your master from leaving in circumstances where he might have become involved in an accident, or lost his licence for drunken driving, he would have been the first to thank you for it, in the morning?'

'I very much doubt it.'

'And you say that you never heard the car go out again.'

'No, I didn't hear it go out again.'

'And of course, we know now that it didn't go out again. You know Mr Morton did not leave the premises again, don't you?'

Ernest sensed the trap and sidestepped at once. 'I don't know it at all.'

'Are you saying that Mr Morton *did* go out again?'

'I am saying that I did not hear him go out again, so I don't know whether he did or not.'

'And yet Mrs Morton and Miss Houseman have told the court that you told them that Mr Morton *had* gone out again.'

'They are mistaken.'

'You are denying that you used those words?'

'I did not use those words.'

'Have you any idea who killed Mr Morton?'

'No.'

'Have you thought about who might have cut the telephone wires?'

'No.'

'But surely, you have been under arrest for eight or nine weeks now, isn't it? And if you did not commit these acts, then someone else must have done and you must surely have given some thought to who that person is?'

'No.'

'Somebody shot Mr Morton. Now is it perhaps your idea that some lover of Mrs Morton, who disliked her husband, might have come to the farm that night, cut the telephone wires, shot her husband and then set fire to the place?'

'I have no idea what happened.'

'But that *might* have been what happened? It's a reasonable idea, is it not? It might have happened that way?'

Ernest spoke reluctantly. He had been seemingly hours in the witness box by now and had never felt so weary. A hard day's work on the farm had never taken such a toll as standing before these folk in their bat-black cloaks, answering question after question. 'I suppose that might have been what happened.'

'You are such a person are you not?' Paley Scott's silky persuasiveness gave way to something verging on triumphant. 'You did love Mrs Morton. You were her lover, were you not?'

'Not by that time, no.'

The judge, who had been quietly noting the questions and replies, now leaned forward and enquired, almost as of a friend: 'Did you ever love her?'

Ernest considered this carefully for a moment, before replying. 'No, I don't think so.'

'But you were jealous,' Mr Paley Scot persisted. 'You disliked her associating with other men.'

'No, that is not so.'

The prosecuting barrister made another of his periodic leaps from one subject to another. 'What time was it, when you got the gun from the kitchen?'

'I'm not sure. Probably about nine o'clock.'

'Why is it that the women did not see you take the gun from the cupboard?'

'They were not in the kitchen the whole time.'

'Why was the gun outside for such a long time?'

'By the time I had fetched it out, the rats were no longer in sight. Rats don't sit around waiting to be shot at.'

'Can you explain why the women only heard one shot, when you say that you fired two?'

'No. I assume they are mistaken.'

'But if you fired one shot in the yard, then another in the mistal, which opens off the yard, those shots would have been clearly audible in the kitchen?'

Ernest said nothing.

'Whereas it is not always possible to hear a shot when it is fired in the garage, is it? Superintendent Blacker and one of his men experimented by firing a shot gun several times in the garage, and not all those shots were audible in the house, were they?'

'I have no idea. I had already been arrested by then.'

'So if you had fired one shot in the garage, the women might not have heard it in the house?'

'I did not fire a shot anywhere near the garage. I fired one shot in the mistal and the other in the yard.'

'I believe you told us that you left the dog, a Great Dane, tied up in its kennel that night?'

'I did.'

'Did you hear the dog bark at all, that night? To give warning of the approach of a stranger, perhaps?'

'I never heard the dog bark any night. It didn't bark very often at all, probably because it was used to hearing small noises made by the horses and cattle moving about and such like.'

'I'd like to return to the matter of the telephone,' said Mr Paley Scot, whose interest in the instrument in question was apparently boundless. 'You have heard witness after witness testify to the fact that a telephone call was made to Saxton Grange at twenty minutes to ten that evening, and yet you have said that you did not hear the telephone ring at all that night.'

'That's correct.'

'How can you explain that?'

'If I was out in the mistal, I wouldn't hear the telephone bell ring in the drawing room, and I probably wouldn't hear it if I was up in the attic, either.'

'Mrs Morton has told the court that you should not have gone up to the attic without permission.'

'That's news to me. I had been up there plenty of times before without seeking permission, to fetch down harnesses and such like when they were needed, and nothing had ever been said about it.'

'And it was during this problem you were experiencing with one of the horses, that you needed to borrow a knife from the kitchen.'

'Yes.'

'Quite a coincidence, isn't it? You are outside with a knife, cutting a piece of rope, just at exactly the same time as someone else must have been outside, with a knife, cutting the telephone wires?'

'I don't know anything about when the telephone wires were cut.'

'And this episode with the head collar, out in the stables, wasn't this also when you cut your thumb?'

'Yes.'

'Why did you not mention cutting your thumb, when you went back to the kitchen?'

'It wasn't worth mentioning. It was only a trivial thing – a little nick. I didn't even notice that I'd done it, until a few minutes afterwards.'

'And you did not mention the problem with the horse which had broken its head collar either, did you? Why was that?'

'It wasn't *a problem*.' Ernest favoured his tormentor with the countryman's look of contempt for the sort of man to whom a lively horse in a darkened stable might well have presented a problem. 'I didn't mention it, because I didn't think they would be interested.'

'You have told the court that the women did not appear to you to be nervous that night. Do you still stand by that statement?'

'I do.'

'You are telling us that neither Miss Houseman, nor Mrs Morton appeared nervous to you at all?'

'That's correct. Mrs Morton was sat sewing. I don't think anybody would be sat there sewing, if they were nervous.'

'Why did you ask Miss Houseman to go out of the room, so that you could talk to Mrs Morton alone?'

'I wanted to tell Mrs Morton about the cow. It was a business matter which had nothing to do with Miss Houseman.'

'Really?' Mr Paley Scot paused, to chuckle theatrically. 'You wanted Miss Houseman to leave you alone, in order to talk about a cow? Was this your idea of a secret business matter?'

Ernest did not waver. 'Yes.'

The judge leaned forward slightly, as he always did, when about to interrupt. 'Do you really mean that?'

'Well the cow was not a secret,' Ernest said carefully. 'But Mrs Morton was a director of the firm and I wouldn't want to discuss any business matters in front of Miss Houseman. She was new at the farm and had nothing to do with the business, so far as I knew.'

'Why did you tell Miss Houseman that it would be better for her if she left the room?'

'I don't believe I said anything of the sort.'

'Can you explain why Miss Houseman and Mrs Morton say that they both heard you use those words?'

'I think they must have either misheard, or misunderstood.'

'Why do you think Miss Houseman refused to leave the room?'

'I supposed that she didn't want to leave the jam.'

'And why did she ask you to give her the shot gun?'

'I have no idea. I offered it to her when she asked for it, but she declined to take it, so I carried on cleaning it and then I put it away.'

'Are you seriously trying to tell this court that you could not see that these two women were terrified of you?'

'They were not terrified.'

'Were you not playing a part, in order to keep them terrified?'

'No.'

'Was there not something outside that you were determined that they should not see?'

'No. I did nothing to stop them from going outside. If I had wanted to keep them in the house, I should not have left them alone. As it was, I was going in and out the whole time and they were free to do the same.'

'So you continue to insist that there was nothing unusual in the women's behaviour at all that night?'

Ernest remained silent. It was becoming a conscious effort not to sway on his feet.

Mr Paley Scot pursued the point relentlessly. 'Can you think of any reason why these two women did not undress, when they went upstairs to bed that night?'

'No.'

'Or why they did not retire to bed, but stayed awake, watching the yard?'

'No.'

'Quite a mystery, isn't it?'

When Ernest said nothing, Paley Scott tried a different question: 'Have you ever had a quarrel with Miss Houseman?'

'No. I hardly know the young woman.'

'So as far as you know, she is an ordinary, truthful, young woman?'

'As I said, I hardly know the young lady.'

'No more questions, my lord.'

In spite of his fatigue, Ernest galvanised his legs into action and walked smartly back from the witness stand to the dock. He was damned if he would let that poncy bugger in the wig get the better of him.

CHAPTER TWELVE

Thursday 14 December 1933
Leeds, Yorkshire

The Black Maria jerked to a standstill, held up again by the late afternoon traffic. From his position on the hard bench seat, Ernest could see very little of the passing world through the high barred windows, but he guessed that perhaps a tram had stopped ahead of them, or else maybe there was some other obstruction in the road ahead. He knew that they had stopped opposite a poulterer's shop, because he could see the game birds hung up outside, still in their feathers, and just above them, the start of the shop sign, PRE, in swirly gold writing, the letters edged with black against a dark blue or green background – hard to tell which by the light thrown onto it from a nearby street lamp. He did not know Leeds well enough to recognise which street they were on, though he was now familiar enough with the journey to be aware that they were still nearer to the Town Hall than to the jail. He felt the prison van edge forward another couple of yards, then stop again. The view from the window changed to a sooty brick wall, unrelieved by anything except a drainpipe.

'Did you ever love her?'

The judge's question came back to him unexpectedly. A funny thing for him to ask, Ernest thought. A dried up old stick like that asking about love. He'd thought about it before he gave his answer, because he wanted to play fair. He had certainly told Dolly that he loved her, because that was what women expected and wanted to hear, when you held them in your arms, but he very much doubted that she had ever really believed him. Dolly had known what she wanted and so had he. It had not been love.

He had always known that what they were doing was wrong. They had both been married to other people when it began, but the Devil had put temptation in his way and when it came in the form of Dolly Morton, offering herself on a plate, as it were, he had never even considered resisting. He had never had a woman like Dolly, smelling of expensive soap, and wearing silk drawers.

It had been a big mistake to ever become involved with her, of course he realised that now. They were different, women of her class – they played by different rules. He had known from the first that she would not stay faithful to him alone, guessing that she not only had an intimate relationship with her own husband, but also with other lovers too. He hadn't troubled over much about that. It was not as if he had expected their affair to last forever, in fact he had always assumed that Dolly would lose interest in him, sooner or later. He represented what a woman like her would refer to as 'a fling'. Besides which, after Mary had been dead a little while, he had begun to think that perhaps it would be nice to marry again and he had made up his mind that if he found the right girl and settled down with her, he would play it straight from then on. He liked the idea of a steady marriage and a proper home. Bachelorhood was over-rated. He was only thirty five and no man wants to end his days living on his Jack Jones in a converted chicken shed.

He had started a bit of a flirtation with young Joan Fletcher in Towton, but as soon as Dolly got to hear of it, she had raised Cain. He had not expected her to be so jealous. After that he had transferred his affections to Ada, the nice young widow who ran a tobacconist shop in Tadcaster. She'd lost her husband to an accident on a farm out Church Fenton way, and had a young lad about the same age as Ethel. He'd taken to calling in at the shop regularly and had stopped to chat to her a few times and given her the kind of looks that let a lass know that a man is interested. She'd not given any sign that this was unwelcome, but matters had gone no further, by the time that he was arrested.

Mr Hyams had suggested bringing these women into court, to testify to his interest in them. It would prove that he was no longer obsessed by Dolly Morton, he had said. Ernest had growled back that he had never been obsessed with Dolly Morton in the first place, and had flatly refused to have his solicitor approach either woman, for they were both respectable and if their names got mixed up in the case folk would only talk. It wasn't fair to drag them into something like this and besides which there had been little enough that either of them could have said. It was not as if he'd been seriously courting them.

Of course it had been a mistake to tell Dolly that he had been taking an interest in another woman, however innocently. She had taken it as a personal insult – him thinking that he might so much as look at a farm labourer's widow, after he'd had her! It had been an even bigger mistake to mention that perhaps, in time, he could find a cottage nearby and make a home there for himself, with a new young wife, and Ethel brought out to join them in the country. Dolly hadn't liked the sound of that at all and sharp words had been exchanged. It was all right for her to keep a string of stallions at her beck and call, but she'd soon got jealous when she thought that his attentions were straying elsewhere.

Ernest was so lost in thought that when the van moved off again, he almost slid off his narrow wooden seat and onto the floor. Whatever the hold-up it had been resolved and the vehicle began its steady crawl through the streets again. As he watched the buildings go by, Ernest thought back over the proceedings of the day. He had put up a good show in the witness box, Mr Hyams had told him. Mr Hyams seemed sure that he would get off. Well of course he would. They couldn't disprove anything that he'd said. The ordeal – probably some form of divine punishment for the undoubtedly bad things which he had done in the past – would soon be over. Tomorrow the jury would hear the final speeches from both sides and then the judge's summing up, and after that they would give their verdict and it would all be over. That's what Mr Hyams said.

The sight of those birds, strung up with their necks wrung and their heads lolling came back into his mind. It was not an omen, he told himself, because he didn't believe in omens and anyway providing that those fellows on the jury had been listening carefully to everything, they would see that there wasn't enough evidence against him to hang a cat.

CHAPTER THIRTEEN

Friday 15 December 1933
Leeds Town Hall, The Yorkshire Assizes

Mr Streatfield addressed the jury in the calm, clear tone of a man who asks of them no more than that they be reasonable. There was no doubt he said, that someone had shot Mr Frederick Morton, and it seemed highly likely that this same person who had shot the master of Saxton Grange, was also the person who had cut the telephone wires and set fire to the garage. The prosecution would have them believe that this person was his client, Ernest Brown.

'It is the task of the prosecution to bring this crime home to Ernest Brown, but this they have most assuredly failed to do. Proof is needed, gentleman, proof beyond reasonable doubt, that it was Ernest Brown who fired the fatal shot, Ernest Brown who cut the telephone wires and Ernest Brown who set fire to the garage.'

As he allowed his words to settle in the air, Mr Streatfield moved a little closer to the jury, creating an almost confidential air. 'You have heard the witness, Mr Cawood, telling you that Frederick Morton left his mother's inn at around a quarter to nine on the night of Tuesday 5 September. In spite of much diligent enquiry by the Yorkshire constabulary, no one knows where Mr Morton went after that. All three of the witnesses who were at the farm that night, Mrs Morton, Miss Houseman and Ernest Brown himself, have told you that no one arrived at the farm by motor car until approximately half past eleven, and Ernest Brown has told you that the person who arrived at half past eleven was Mr Morton.

'Again, all three of the witnesses who were at the farm that night have told you that by half past eleven that night, Ernest Brown had cleaned the only gun on the premises, and replaced it in the kitchen cupboard, where it was found the next morning. It therefore stands to reason that if Frederick Morton was shot shortly after arriving home, Ernest Brown cannot possibly have been the guilty party, since the only weapon available to him was shut in a cupboard, in full view of two witnesses who did not see him take it out.

'Gentlemen of the jury, I put it to you that the prosecution have not provided a shred of evidence which shows that it was Ernest Brown who fired the fatal shot that night. Irrespective of whether Mr Morton left the premises again, as he had suggested that he would to Ernest Brown, or whether he remained in the garage, perhaps sleeping in his car, as he had done on more than one occasion in the past, it would appear far more likely that some other person, possibly someone who had brought along their own gun for the purpose, was responsible for the shot which killed him.

'Dr Sutherland has told you that any person who shot Frederick Morton at close range would be very likely to have blood on his clothes, yet my client, who had no opportunity to change his clothes at any point that evening, and who was still wearing those exact same clothes the following day, right up until his arrest, had no blood on him, save for a tiny amount which as his lordship has rightly pointed out, could have got on there at any time, in the ordinary course of his working life.'

Mr Streatfield retreated momentarily, for a sip of water from the ever ready glass on his table, before continuing. The jury must ask themselves, he said, whether it was really likely that Mrs Morton could determine, by the light of the single oil lamp which was burning in the kitchen that night, the colour of the handle of a knife, taken from a drawer in a dresser which stood on the opposite side of the room to where she was sitting.

'Why would she even have taken any notice of such a detail? You have heard from Ernest Brown that he had frequently used the black handled knife, which you see here in court, ever since mislaying his own pocket knife, several weeks before. It was a routine thing. He has told you that the horse, whose head collar he needed to replace, had often broken free before – another routine matter – an occurrence so ordinary, that he did not even think it worth mentioning, when the three occupants of the kitchen were chatting, later that evening.

'I wish to particularly draw your attention to this period during which the three witnesses sat talking together, in the kitchen. Gentlemen, does this sound to you like a situation in which one man has recently shot another? Having finished his chores for the night, Ernest Brown sits in the kitchen, chatting about the everyday business of the farm, just as he does every other night, while his mistress does her sewing, and the young woman employed as a mother's companion, boils up a pan of jam. Mrs Morton and her companion would have you believe that they were terrified of Ernest Brown and of what he might do to them, but when asked to provide examples of this so-called terrifying behaviour, they can only tell the court that Ernest Brown merely sat and talked to them, in a perfectly normal, ordinary way.'

Ernest stole a look at the jury to see how they were taking all this and noticed that the thin faced chap, who always sat at the end of the bench nearest to the dock was surreptitiously picking something out of his teeth. Was that a good sign or not? Perhaps he had already made up his mind in Ernest's favour, but all the same, Ernest wished that the fellow would sit up straight and give his full attention to what Mr Streatfield was saying.

'Earlier on that evening, Brown asks his mistress's help in shutting up some ducks for the night, and she declines to give it. Does he immediately lose his temper, this man who is supposedly so "mad", so "wild"? Does he start to threaten and bluster? Not at all. He accepts her excuse and goes outside to do the job himself. When he returns the shotgun to the kitchen, does he threaten the women with it? He does not. Indeed when Miss Houseman asks him to hand her the gun, he is perfectly willing to do so. In what way does any of this constitute threatening – nay terrifying – behaviour?

'This is a man who has spent his entire evening going about his chores, seeing to the stock, stoking the boiler, replacing a horse's harness when it was needed. For Ernest Brown, this has been just another ordinary night on the farm. If something was troubling Mrs Morton, then he was unaware of it.'

Mr Streatfield paused, as if allowing the jury to consider the point. He took another sip from his water. From somewhere in the public gallery, came a fait, rasping squeak, of boot leather scraping against boot leather, as someone fidgeted their cramped legs and feet.

'Consider the reaction of Ernest Brown, on realising that the garage was ablaze. His first thought was for the animals. At not inconsiderable risk to himself, he entered the buildings nearest to the inferno, and made certain that every last horse and cow was saved. This, gentlemen, is surely the act of a loyal servant, a true countryman, not that of a maniac, intent on murdering his employer and destroying his farm. With the animals safe, he attempted to telephone for assistance, and when that failed, he drove into the nearest village, sounding the horn in order to get help as quickly as possible. In the meantime, for reasons best known to themselves, his employer's wife and her companion had fled the premises.

'Gentlemen, Ernest Brown's fate rests with you today. It has been suggested that he is a jealous man, that he is a violent man, who forced Mrs Morton to become intimate with him, and forced her to continue in this state of intimacy – against her will – for a period of several years. Saxton Grange was a busy place, employing numerous people, and visited by many more, yet the prosecution has not produced one single witness willing to testify to this strange – one might say, this incredible – state of affairs which allegedly existed between Ernest Brown and the wife of his master. Mrs Morton's supposed great and longstanding fear of Ernest Brown, rests upon her testimony alone. Even if it were the case that Ernest Brown was jealous of the attentions being paid to Mrs

Morton by *several* other men, what possible reason did this give him for shooting her husband that night? Apart from a couple of remarks, made in jest, there is no evidence at all, of any animosity between Ernest Brown and his employer. On the contrary, they were on unusually friendly terms, with the man Brown being accustomed to address his employer by his Christian name. They had known one another for a very long time and there was no animosity between them.

'I put it to you that there is not a shred of evidence that this man in the dock before you, shot his late employer. Gentlemen, there is no lack of suspects in this case. Jealous lovers, and disgruntled customers alike. *Anyone* might have arrived at some point that evening, lain in wait until the time was ripe, committed the deed, set fire to the buildings and then made good his escape, perhaps by means of a motor car parked a couple of fields away, or even just a quarter mile or so down the lane. My learned friend is unable to state with any certainty, either the hour at which Frederick Morton was killed, or whether the bullet felled him as he sat in his motor car, or whether he was killed elsewhere and his body then placed in the motor car. He cannot be certain which gun was used to fire the fatal shot, whether there was a single cartridge fired, or more than one. He has completely and utterly failed to bring this dreadful crime home to the man who stands on trial before you today'

As Mr Streatfield resumed his seat Ernest experienced a surge of confidence. Surely anyone could see that there was a lack of hard evidence against him? But as Mr Paley Scot rose to make his final address to the jury, the expression on the prosecuting barrister's face sent an icy sliver of doubt into his mind. It was much the same as the one which Paley Scott had adopted at the outset of his own cross examination, confident, as befits a man who knows that he has the upper hand. He watched as Mr Paley Scot took the couple of steps necessary to cross the floor and take up the position from which he could best address the jury.

'Gentlemen, the fact of the matter is, that on Tuesday 5 September this year, someone took a gun and used it to shoot Frederick Morton in the heart. Later that night, this same person set fire to the garage at Saxton Grange, hoping that the body would be completely destroyed and the death mistakenly attributed to an accident. But the killer was unlucky. Fate took a hand, gentlemen, and though much of Mr Morton's body was destroyed, the portion of his chest in which the shot had lodged was preserved – in such a way that it will be possible to bring the perpetrator to justice. It does not matter whether this dreadful act occurred when Mr Morton was sitting inside or standing outside his motor car, or even at precisely what hour the fatal shot was fired. The important question is, whose hand was on the trigger of the shotgun?

'The defence in this case has envisaged the existence of some sort of phantom lover. A mysterious, unidentified person who managed to arrive at the farm that night without anyone seeing or hearing him. A man at whom the guard dog does not bark. A man who uses a knife from the kitchen drawer – which he has somehow managed to obtain without being seen by the two women who are sitting in the kitchen the whole time, or by the manservant who is moving around between the kitchen and the yard – and this mysterious person cuts the telephone wires, and by some unaccountable coincidence, he does this at around the exact same time that Ernest Brown claims he was using a completely different knife from that same kitchen drawer, to cut a rope in the stables.

'The only person seen to handle a gun at Saxton Grange that night was Ernest Brown, who when asked for an explanation for the shot heard by the women in the house, came up with a ridiculous story about shooting at some rats. Are we to seriously believe that a man who has spent so many years in service on a farm, would waste his time, blasting away at rats, with the dusk fast falling? That shot had a much more sinister purpose, gentlemen, and the victim was not a rat, but Mr Frederick Morton, who on his arrival home that night, met with a violent death at the hand of a man who had more than once threatened to do him harm.

'The defence has attempted to paint a picture of an ordinary night, in which the man in the dock, Ernest

Brown, engages only in perfectly ordinary things. Gentlemen of the jury, put yourselves now in the place of these two young women. Picture that lonely house, with only one lamp burning, as the hour grows later and later, and they await the long delayed arrival of Mr Morton. Their home has been transformed into a place of mystery and terror. Brown's eyes were wild, his demeanour mad. First the women heard a shot ring out, and soon afterwards, the man Brown was seen fetching a knife from the drawer. Is it any wonder that these women were terrified of him, fearing all the time what he might do next?

'You have seen the considerable courage exhibited by these women, as they told their story to the court. Was the whole of Mrs Morton and Miss Houseman's evidence a pack of lies? Mrs Morton has stood before you and admitted that she was not always a faithful wife, but because Mrs Morton had been unfaithful, this does not mean that she cannot be believed.

'Members of the jury, you have heard the evidence and I put it to you that there is only one logical interpretation of it all. The man who shot Frederick Morton that night is the man in the dock before you. In the name of justice, I must ask you to bring in a guilty verdict against Ernest Brown.'

CHAPTER FOURTEEN

Friday 15 December 1933
Leeds Town Hall, The Yorkshire Assizes

'You don't fancy another game of cards, or anything, Ernest?'

It was a pity, Ernest thought, that the regulations didn't allow them to play for money, because he would have made a fortune out of Bottomley and Jordan, the two warders who had been assigned to accompany him to and fro from the prison for most of the hearings, first at the magistrates' courts and now at the assizes. Of course it had occurred to him once or twice that they might be letting him win, because they felt sorry for him and thought him likely to hang, but he had pushed the thought away, and in any case he did not think that either man was capable of dealing a crooked hand. A pack of cards had often helped them to while away the time they had spent just waiting around, but it didn't seem fitting to play just now – not with a dozen men somewhere close by, deliberating upon his fate. Besides which, the sensation in the pit of his stomach would have proved too much of a distraction – it would have been impossible to fully focus on the cards.

It was a good sign that they were taking their time, Ernest thought, because then there has to have been a discussion. It was not unknown for a jury in a murder case, having listened to several days of testimony, to take no more than twenty minutes to decide that the man in the dock was guilty. Five minutes to make up their minds and have a vote on it, and the other quarter hour to have a quick cup of tea and smoke a pipe, so one of the warders had said.

It was very quiet, sitting alongside the familiar guards, with whom he had declined to play the usual games of whist, during the hour or more that they had been sitting in the little tiled cell, beneath the court room. You couldn't hear anything down there. Not from the court room, or the teeming streets outside. There might have been nothing else going on in the world, though with Christmas fast approaching, Ernest knew that the streets would be packed with people. He pictured the crowds and the excited faces of the kiddies. Imagined the lights shining out of the frosted glass windows of the pubs, and the bursts of laughter from every doorway.

Smells from the hawkers with their chestnuts, roasting atop street corner braziers. Fried fish from the fish shops, the cries of the newspaper vendors, the clang and trundle of the trams. Never again would he take any of that for granted.

Soon now, he would be going home to stay at his mother's – the worry of the last few weeks erased from her face. Probably all the family waiting to greet him, and little Ethel, running to him with her arms outstretched. By God, he hoped they'd managed to keep all this business from her.

He knew he would be going home, because that was what the law said. For a man to be found guilty of murder, the jury must be sure of their verdict, beyond reasonable doubt – and they could not possibly be. He would walk from the court a free man. People in the street would come up and want to shake his hand. They might even cheer him, when he came out of the front door and down those steps out front. He'd read about such things happening, in the newspapers.

'They're ready.'

The announcement at the door generated a scramble of activity, for though they had been tensely awaiting the summons, now it had suddenly come, it was a bit of a rush to get back up into the court.

It was a relief, Ernest told himself, that this was the last time he would have to come up those stairs, the last time the whole cast of the circus would reassemble. The judge in his ridiculous robes and his wig. A horrible old bastard, Ernest thought, who had certainly not summed up in his favour – but all the same, all the same, the jury could not possibly find him guilty, because it had to be beyond reasonable doubt. The barristers, with their smaller wigs, each finished off with a little white tail at the back, not pointing straight down, but curling away, forced into shape by repeated contact with the wearer's collar or shoulders. Mr Paley Scott's had reminded him of a curly pig's tail. The old biddies, who would have to get off home to their shopping and their laundry, their little bit of excitement over and done until the next assizes rolled around.

From force of habit, he did not look across at the jury, but he allowed himself a glance at the bench in the well of the court, where Dolly had been allowed to sit alongside her father day by day, listening to the case, and he realised that she and her little entourage were missing. Didn't want the press to see her face, he supposed, when the jury brought in a verdict that made her look a liar. Even so, her unaccustomed absence gave him an uncomfortable jolt.

When the order came for him to stand, he stood at attention in the dock, his shoulders squared.

'Gentlemen of the jury, do you find the prisoner, Ernest Brown, guilty or not guilty?'

The foreman was on his feet. And suddenly everything was happening in slow motion. The verdict given, a gasp from the public gallery, followed by what sounded like a scuffle of some kind. The fellow who had announced the verdict was glaring across at him, as venomous as if it had been his own son, whose life had been taken.

Now the judge was addressing him, in a hard cold voice, asking if he had anything to say, before sentence was passed. Ernest hesitated. He ran his tongue around his lips and looked down again, at the empty place, until recently occupied by Dolly. Then he gave the slightest shake of his head.

'Ernest Brown, you have been found guilty of a cruel and brutal murder. I think it is only right to say that I agree with the verdict.'

Though his eyes remained fixed on the judge, the man in the dock saw not the face of Travers Humphreys, nor the shining coat of arms behind his head, nor even the square of black cloth, as it was placed atop that ridiculous wig, but the blindingly bright, orange and yellow flames as they leaped from the roof of the garage, and the sinister outline of the Chrysler car which stood inside, as the fire consumed the mortal remains of Frederick Morton.

CHAPTER FIFTEEN

Martin's Nest

Holywell Green

Yorkshire

6 January 1934

To the Governor, His Majesty's Prison, Armley, Leeds.

Dear Sir,

I am writing on behalf of myself and my father to ask whether it would be possible to require Ernest Brown, currently under sentence of death for the murder of my brother, Frederick Ellison Morton, to provide a blood sample, which could be checked against a sample from Mrs Morton's daughter, Diana Morton, in order to establish whether or not Ernest Brown is the father of this child. This knowledge would help to put our minds at rest.

Yours sincerely

Florence Ellison Morton

His Majesty's Prison, Armley, Leeds
10 January 1934

Dear Miss Morton,

Regarding the request made in your letter of 6th inst., the Home Secretary wishes me to point out to you that since the child may have inherited her mother's blood group, and that we are unaware to which blood group your brother, the late Mr Frederick Morton belonged, conducting such a test would not necessarily establish paternity and would therefore not be in the public interest.

Yours sincerely

Thomas Docherty

Governor of His Majesty's Prison, Armley.

CHAPTER SIXTEEN

Tuesday 16 January 1934
Martin's Nest, Holywell Green, Yorkshire

A tap on the dining room door preceded Hilda's entry, but she stopped short on the threshold when she saw that both the master and Miss Florence were still seated at the breakfast table. 'Sorry, sir, sorry mum, I thought you was finished.'

'That's all right, Hilda. We'll only be another few minutes and then you can clear away.'

Hilda retreated and Florence wondered afresh what it was about the girl that she could not take to. There was nothing to complain of in her manner, or the way in which she carried out her duties. 'If she makes you feel uncomfortable,' Aunt Phoebe had said, 'just give her a good character and send her on her way.'

But it wasn't as simple as that, Florence thought. She didn't feel that she could give a servant notice, just because she didn't like her. It seemed unfair and besides which, though she officially ran the house now that her mother was dead, she still deferred to her father in the matter of hiring and firing staff, and that would mean giving him a reason when there really wasn't one.

Aunt Phoebe – who seemed to imagine that they were all still living in an era when good house parlour maids were simply queuing up to work for one – had no such qualms. 'Get rid of her if you don't like her,' she said. 'It's your home Florence, you don't need a better reason than that – and anyway, one's instincts never lie. She's probably stealing or something. Have you accounted for all the teaspoons, dear?'

Florence was abruptly recalled to the present by her father's voice, which emerged from behind his newspaper. 'Brown's appeal has failed.'

'He will hang then.' She was careful to keep her voice neutral. By the time she'd arrived at the breakfast table, her father had already commandeered the morning paper, as was his accustomed habit, folding it in on itself, so that she could not see the front page. She had not interrupted his reading, merely exchanging a "Good morning" when she entered the room and then maintaining their usual silence during the meal, since her father had never liked idle chatter over breakfast.

She had guessed of course, that the result of Brown's appeal would be in the morning paper, but her dilemma over Hilda had made her temporarily forget about it. This surprised her, even came as a shock, because it had certainly been the uppermost question in her mind when she came downstairs that morning, and she had continued to think about it throughout the time it had taken her to butter a slice of toast, then coat it thinly with home-made marmalade, before forcing her mouth to nibble at the slice until it was all gone. Sometimes it felt as if she had thought of nothing else but Freddie's death, the circumstances of it and the arrest and trial of the groom, ever since the news about poor Freddie had been telephoned through to them, on that Wednesday morning back in September, when they had been sitting down to breakfast, just as they were today. Yet now, almost four long months later, with the crucial news from London expected, the whole thing had completely slipped from her mind. The appeal had failed and Ernest Brown would hang.

It was not just her father's general dislike of breakfast time conversation which had held her back from enquiring whether Brown was to be spared. She knew that her father's wounds were still raw, and that any conversation touching upon the loss of his son exacerbated the pain, but since it was he who had raised the news, she decided to risk pursuing the issue.

'I hear there is a substantial petition,' she ventured. 'His family must hope even now for a reprieve.'

'There's always a petition in these cases.' The newspaper remained in place. 'A reprieve is most unlikely.'

'I should like to visit him again.'

'My dear Flossie, what on earth good do you think that would do?' The newspaper descended at last and her father faced her across the table. 'He'll not change his story now.'

'I can't believe that it can just be left at this,' her voice rose in spite of her best intentions. 'It must have been obvious, even to a child, that the whole truth had not been told.'

'It isn't the job of the court to bring out the whole truth,' her father said. 'Establishing guilt or innocence is enough for them.'

'I heard some women talking in a tea shop in town. They're saying that it's common knowledge in Huddersfield that some important evidence was not heard. Evidence which would have helped Ernest Brown.'

'I don't believe there's anything to be gained from listening to a lot of loose talk and gossip in town.' He twitched the paper back into place and turned a page.

Florence was tempted to retort that she did not think there was anything to be gained from hiding away in one's study, with a whiskey decanter for company every night, but she had never spoken to her father in such a fashion and thought it unlikely that she ever would.

'But surely, Daddy, you aren't satisfied that the whole truth came out?'

'You know that I'm not. Any more than the public were. I won't forget in a hurry that baying mob, waiting outside the Town Hall for Dorothy and that silly young thing who supported her, after the verdict had been announced. The police tried to take them out of the back door, but the mob second guessed them and split up – one pack taking the front of the building, with the others posted round at the rear. In the end, they had to get a line of policemen to link arms, but it was as much as they could do to keep the crowd back, when they hustled those two women down to the car, with two big burly peelers, one on either side of each of them. Even then the crowd tried to press round the car. The man who was driving ran the car straight at the crowd to make them get out of the way – fellow might easily have run someone down.'

'There you are. Those people knew that Dorothy wasn't telling all.'

'Perhaps they just didn't like the kind of woman that Dorothy is.'

There were certain words that her father would not use in front of her, Florence thought. Words which would sum up very succinctly, the kind of woman Dorothy was. They had, of course, discussed the possibility that Freddie had not been the father of Dorothy's child, but it had been an awkward little conversation, laced with euphemisms, which had skirted around the main issue, taking care not to touch on any improprieties. With her father's agreement, she had written to the Home Office, asking about a blood test, but the negative response had left them in an ambivalent position. Poor Daddy had initially been so proud of the little girl he had called his grandchild, whereas now he seriously doubted that she was of his blood at all. It seemed perfectly likely that Ernest Brown, or even some other man, could have been little Diana's father. The child which had initially appeared to represent their one tangible link with Freddie, had become almost a source of embarrassment; a cuckoo in the nest.

When she had asked Brown himself the question, during her first visit to the jail: 'Is there any chance that you, rather than Freddie, are the little girl's father?' He had replied, 'Well Dolly says that I am.'

Perhaps, she thought, he has reconsidered his position, since I visited him last. At that time Brown had still hoped to have his conviction overturned, but surely now that the appeal had been rejected, he had nothing to gain from withholding the full story? Her father had not signified his approval for a second visit, but neither had he forbidden it. She was of age, of course, but that was a technicality – she would not have gone against him, if he had made an outright refusal. Since he had not, she decided that she would write to the prison authorities again.

CHAPTER SEVENTEEN

Wednesday 17 January 1934
His Majesty's Prison, Armley, Yorkshire

'Then the chap says, "I don't like your attitude" and the other fellow says "It's not my hat he chewed, it's your hat he chewed."' Entwhistle finished his joke with a great guffaw of laughter, and Albert Henshaw joined in.

'Aye,' he said cheerfully. 'It's a good 'un.'

He had heard the joke before, but he was happy enough to humour Will Entwhistle, who might not have been the shiniest penny in the purse, but was a big, bruiser of a fellow and always a good man to have at your back if there was any sign of trouble. Entwhistle stretched out his long legs under the table and reached for his newly-made mug of tea. Albert took out his handkerchief and blew his nose loudly. There were a lot of colds and coughs going about and he hoped that he wasn't going down with one. Both men looked up as Joe Fazackerley entered the mess room.

'There's a brew just made,' Entwhistle called out, the echoes of laughter still present in his voice. 'And how is your charge taking things, now that yon appeal's been turned down?'

'I can't say as I've noticed any change.' Fazackerley did not turn his head, no doubt concentrating on the management of the huge enamel teapot, which he had lifted from the hotplate in order to help himself to a mug of thick brown tea. 'He still seems to think that he'll get off in the end.'

Entwhistle shook his head. 'No confession yet then?'

'He says he's innocent.'

'Well tell me something new.' Entwhistle paused to take a gulp of his steaming tea, but withdrew his lips hastily, exclaiming, 'By heck, that's still scalding, that is!' before reverting to his original mocking tone and adding: 'Whole bloody place is full of innocent men, as we all well know.'

Albert watched in silence, as Fazackerley began to stir some lump sugar into his brew, chinking the spoon around and around the thick pottery mug, while the stuff took forever to dissolve. He could tell from the stiffness of Fazackerley's shoulders that Entwhistle was getting on his nerves. Always a bit of a bull in a china shop, was Will Entwhistle.

'Happen this one is innocent.' Fazackerley's tone, unlike Entwhistle's, was completely devoid of merriment or sarcasm.

'What's that supposed to mean?' Entwhistle asked. 'Jury found him guilty. That's the beginning and end of it, so far as we're concerned in here.'

Albert looked from one man to the other, conscious of mounting tension in the air. The Prison Service was very much like it had been in the army. They were all a band of brothers in here and it did not do to break ranks. Prisoners were on one side and they were on the other and while there was no harm in treating the other side with a degree of respect, you couldn't ever afford to forget on which side of the divide you stood.

'The padre thinks he's innocent,' Fazackerley said quietly. 'And for all that he's a man of God, he's nobody's fool.'

'Then he'll get a shock when t'bloke confesses, the night before they take him on his last walk down to the Topping Shed.' Entwhistle blew on his mug, before taking another slug of his tea.

Fazackerley was still working the spoon in a circular motion, chinking it repeatedly against the sides of his mug, almost as if he had forgotten what he was doing. 'He won't confess – not this one.'

'Get away… they all confess in the end. That's why the padre keeps popping in on them, trying to convince them that the only hope of saving their immortal souls is to spill the beans, at the last minute – though personally, I reckon such as him will be going straight to hell. A confession won't bring that young feller what he shot back to life, will it?'

'Why don't you give it a rest, Entwhistle?' Albert broke in. 'And for Christ's sake, Joe, quit stirring that blooming tea around. You'll wear out the cup, never mind dissolve the ruddy sugar.'

After a moment or two of silence, Entwhiste said: 'It was a poor do in the cup on Saturday. Fancy Leeds losing to Preston North End – and them only in the second division. Mind you, I reckon they could get promoted, this season. I see Stoke City beat Bradford Park Avenue 3-0. I reckon they could be the dark horses this year. I'm putting a bob on them for the Cup.'

'Get away. They'll not be at Wembley, any more than Leeds United.' Albert was not much of a man for football, much preferring the cricket himself, but he was grateful for Entwhistle's efforts to divert them away from what had had the makings of an awkward confrontation. Small wonder that old Entwhistle – a good enough bloke to have on your side as a general rule – was taken aback by Joe's attitude toward the prisoner, which ran dead against everything they were trained to think. And yet there was something rum about this Brown business, he reflected. Something which made people lose their heads. He thought about the unruly mob which had gathered outside the court in the wake of the verdict. And what was it which had made an otherwise respectable young woman like that Miss Morton come trotting along to visit the man who had been convicted of murdering her own brother? Whatever it was, it had also affected the padre and now the contagion had even spread to an old hand like Joe Fazackerley, who had never been known to espouse a prisoner's innocence before.

'Bit of a surprise when Huddersfield only drew,' Fazackerley said, apparently also glad to seize upon an alternative topic. 'It's the replay at Leeds Road tonight.'

'Plymouth Argyle isn't it?' Entwhistle nodded. 'Long way to come for a thrashing.'

'I reckon so.'

'Where the heck is Plymouth, anyway?' Entwhistle slugged down another gulp of tea, before taking off his cap and giving his close-shorn head a good scratch.

'It's down on the south coast,' Albert said. 'Beyond Bristol and Exeter.'

'Right.' Entwhistle nodded. 'Never got down that way myself. They'll have no chance against Huddersfield. Not that Huddersfield's the side it was, with Bomber Brown gone and Billy Smith getting to the end of the road. Mind you, they've set records that will never be broken. Three league titles in a row! There won't be another club what does that in a hurry.'

'It was Herbert Chapman that brought them success,' Fazackerley said. 'It was a big surprise, seeing in the papers that he'd died. Only fifty five and all.'

Albert remained silent, content to let the football talk wash over him. Then it occurred to him that Fazackerley was not a Huddersfield man, nor even so far as he knew, all that much interested in football. He wondered if it had been Brown who had drawn his attention to the results, and the unexpected death of the old team manager. Brown was Huddersfield born and bred and in Albert's experience Huddersfield folk had a particular affinity to their team. He thought of Ernest Brown, following the progress of his team in a cup competition whose outcome he was not destined to know. They wouldn't be playing the fourth round until towards the end of February and by that time...

Albert pulled himself up short. It would be a good thing when the whole business was behind them. The jail was always unsettled by an execution. The last one had been a good eighteen months ago – a double hanging, Riley and Roberts, both despatched on the same day. This Brown business had been dragging on since last September and now there was another prisoner awaiting trial and bound to go the same way. Open and shut case, was Louis Hamilton's. Cut his wife's throat on Boxing Day, of all things. Only in their twenties, the pair of them. No mystery about that sort of case and no chance of the poor young woman's relatives dropping in to pay him a visit neither.

CHAPTER EIGHTEEN

Thursday 18 January 1934
Martin's Nest, Holywell Green, Yorkshire

Florence smuggled *The Empire News* into the house as if it were contraband. She had made up her mind to read it in full herself, before she decided whether or not to draw it to her father's notice. He was probably unaware of their advertising. He was not noted for his powers of observation and could easily have missed the words scrawled on the boards outside the newsagents' doorways, when he had driven himself into town the day before. Florence herself would not have been aware of the *Empire News's* scoop, if she had not happened to overhear Hilda talking with Cook about it, in the kitchen that morning: a little bit of inadvertent eavesdropping which had immediately set her inventing an errand which necessitated taking the motor car into Huddersfield, with the intention of buying a copy of the newspaper in question.

It had not been a good day for driving and the car had all but gone into a skid on the top bend of the lane, but she had made it back home safely and with all the doors and windows firmly closed against the winter chill, she thought there was every chance that her arrival had gone unobserved. She let herself in and closed the front door very slowly and quietly. Daddy would be still at the works, and the staff would be busy in the rear of the house at this time of day. She rested the folded newspaper on the hallstand while she slipped off her coat and hung it up, then carefully unlaced her damp-soled, outdoor shoes and left them neatly paired on the polished floor. Her stocking feet made no sound at all on the thick Turkey carpet which ran all the way up the stairs and then in a broad strip along the landing, flanked by yet more polished floorboards – a shiny margin which she and Freddie had once upon a time pretended was water to be jumped across. The imaginary, shiny brook which separated the edge of the nursery rug from the bridge provided by the hall runner had seemed an almost insurmountable distance to them then. How wonderful to have nothing but lessons with Fraulein Schmidt, then half the day to inhabit a world of make believe games, in which floorboards became rivers, the nursery toy chest a pirate galleon, while a hall cupboard was the lair of a terrible dragon which breathed real fire. How unappreciative they had been of it all, how little they had valued those precious, precious times.

Once upstairs, she opened her bedroom door with over-elaborate care, hesitating on the threshold lest the room be occupied. Ridiculous of course, because no one was likely to come in for anything at that time of day, not between Hilda doing the mid-morning dusting, and then returning much later to light the evening fires, and later still to turn down the beds and put the stone hot water bottles in place at nine o'clock each night.

It was cold in the bedroom of course. Even to someone fresh from the wintery garden. There would be a fire in the drawing room and if she went to sit in there, she could ring for a pot of tea, but with that came the possibility of interruption. She did not want Hilda to come fussing in, wanting to poke the fire or remove the tea tray, and in doing so catch sight of her reading this particular paper. Cook and Hilda both knew what was in it today, and Florence knew that they gossiped incorrigibly with every delivery boy and tradesman, with the other servants belonging to the nearby houses, and with their own families too, when they went home on their days off, and she was tired of being the object of their interest and speculation. Hilda in particular, she suspected of disloyalty. Suppose Hilda talked to a newspaper reporter? The papers were capable of printing anything and Florence did not want anyone and everyone to know that she was buying a rag like the *Empire News*, in the hope of learning more about her brother's death. It was undignified.

As for Daddy, she did not want to see his face clouded with worry, or to hear his latest feeble excuse for heading to his study and the consolation of the decanter that stood on the table inside. She knew that her father wanted the matter dropped. Freddie was dead and nothing would bring him back. Pondering the rights and wrongs of it all, considering the possibility that little Diana was not his granddaughter, raking over his son's marital unhappiness, did no more than twist the knife in his wounds. As for the little girl Diana, upon whom he had once set so much store, she was already almost certainly lost to him, for word had come from the Middlemost family that in the wake of the tragedy, Dolly and the child would very likely sell up the cattle factoring business – and probably Saxton Grange with it – and go to live abroad.

'Of course,' Aunt Phoebe had said, in her blunt, blundering way, 'It's very bad form, the property being sold out of the family when it had been specifically left to Freddie, but then one can quite understand that the place would be full of painful memories. Imagine looking out of one's windows every day, and seeing the place where poor dear Freddie died.'

Florence privately thought that with her reputation in ruins, Dolly would need to go somewhere a long, long way from Yorkshire, if she ever wanted to be invited about in polite society again, and that it would be this sort of consideration, rather than any sense of loss or tragedy, which had motivated her sister-in-law to think of selling up and moving away.

Having eschewed the warmth of the drawing room, Florence hesitated for a moment, then hauled the heavy, purplish pink eiderdown off the bed, sat with her legs folded under her on top of the blankets, and wrapped herself up in the shiny, quilted satin. To begin with it felt icy next to her skin, but she knew that it would only take a few minutes before its weight brought a welcome warmth to her body.

Nestled within the confines of the quilt, she opened the newspaper at last and turned the pages until she found what she was looking for. Entitled 'The Night of Terror at Saxton Grange', the paper promised that the piece was an exclusive, penned by 'the heroine of these events', Miss Ann Houseman.

Florence read on with mounting indignation, wondering as she did, how much money the paper had paid that odious little mouse to write it. She supposed that the editor felt able to publish Ann Houseman's story, now that Ernest Brown's appeal had failed, yet there was something disgusting in the way that it had appeared within a mere twenty four hours of the higher court's decision, something sordid in the gleeful exploitation of a story – still not quite at its conclusion – which had begun with the death of one man and was destined to end in the death of another. Florence thought that the very paper felt contaminated between her fingers, as she turned the sheets in order to follow the story across several columns, which were located on successive pages.

How the newspapers twisted things, she thought. According to the preamble, the full story of the night's events was being told for the first time by Miss Houseman, who had 'faithfully protected her mistress during their six hour ordeal at the hands of a madman'. As if Ann Houseman, that silly little ninny, would ever be capable of protecting anyone from anything! According to the *Empire News*, Miss Houseman's original words had been reproduced without alteration. Presumably Miss Houseman had been able to name her price and stipulate her own conditions, Florence thought, no doubt the little fool imagined that she had a gift for writing. As she read on, barely able to suppress her indignation, the experience was rendered infinitely more painful by the author's cringe-worthy, schoolgirl compulsion for over-description. How the editor's pen hand must have twitched, Florence thought. Saxton Grange itself was portrayed in detail, together with the grounds and the surrounding countryside, in which 'contented cows pass their peaceful hours' while 'the silver pond smiles back its light to the blue heaven.'

Though the paper had promised that it would be 'the full story' for 'the first time', so far as Florence could tell, the tale which Ann Houseman presented to the readers of *The Empire News* was much the same as that which she and Dorothy had been telling all along. As she continued to work her way through the morass of Ann Houseman's verbiage, Florence was struck anew by the improbability of it all. In court it had emerged gradually, a series of answers in response to carefully phrased questions, whereas here it was presented as a coherent narrative, which made it sound all the more like a plot from a tuppenny novelette in which the villain behaves like a raving madman, while the helpless womenfolk show less gumption than a bunch of chickens in a coop.

'It isn't true,' Florence murmured, as she read. 'I just know it isn't true.'

Dolly was such a persuasive character, Florence thought. You had only to recall the way Freddie had fallen under her spell, even pretending to be older than he was, in order to more closely match her years. Dolly could easily have asked one of her lovers to come by night and remove an increasingly inconvenient husband. Had the jury realised that Freddie had made a will, just a few months before his death, leaving Dolly everything? How much had Ann Houseman known about her mistress's carryings-on with other men? The girl was such a goose, she would no doubt have believed whatever Dolly cared to tell her. She had only been at Saxton Grange a matter of six short weeks when it all happened – not nearly long enough to have got Dolly's measure. Not long enough to have known anything about the affair between her mistress and the man who drove the horsebox, or to have witnessed Ernest Brown's leave taking and return in June. There was probably an awful lot, Florence reflected, that Ann Houseman had not known about Dolly – just as she herself, her father and poor Freddie, had been largely in ignorance of Dolly's temperament and predilections, when they had first encountered her, during Freddie and Dolly's whirlwind courtship, nine years ago.

When she reached the end of the narrative, Florence carefully disentangled herself from the eiderdown, rose from the bed and crossed to the wardrobe, which she opened, reaching to the back of the upper shelf, where she had placed the flat, rectangular shirt box in a corner where the maids would have no reason to go. Having extracted the box and set it on the big walnut dressing table, which took up almost the entire bay window, she opened the second drawer down, where she kept her fountain pen and a sheaf of loose paper. Having assembled these various items, she pulled out the upholstered stool and sat down, carefully moving aside her hairbrushes and the green glass dressing table set in order to make more space. She positioned the pile of writing paper next to the *Empire News*, which was still folded open at the page bearing Ann Houseman's account; unscrewed the cap of her pen, and began to read afresh. After a moment or two, she removed the lid of the shirt box and began to sift through the press cuttings she had folded inside, checking first one and then another until she found the specific items which she sought, breaking off for a moment to fetch the eiderdown and drape it around her shoulders, before resuming where she had left off, reading the account in *The Empire News* line by line, comparing it to the testimony reported from the trial and making methodical notes as she went.

She was interrupted by an urgent tapping on the door and Hilda's voice, from the landing. 'Miss Florence? Miss Florence? Are you all right?'

'Of course I'm all right.' Florence grabbed the various cuttings and began to stuff them back into the box any old how. Hilda had taken her response as permission to enter and was in the act of pushing open the door.

'Your father has come home, Miss Florence. He saw your motor car on the drive and wondered if you'd been taken poorly, seeing as how you'd gone straight up to your room.'

'No, Hilda, I am perfectly well, thank you.' Florence could see curiosity written all over the girl's face.

'Would you like me to light the fire in here, mum?' The girl was looking at the eiderdown.

'No thank you.' Florence attempted dignity. 'You can tell my father that I am coming down in just a moment. Have some tea made and bring it into the drawing room for us, would you please.'

She sensed reluctance in Hilda's withdrawal. Her curiosity had no doubt been aroused and she would surely mull the matter over with cook, but Florence was confident that the wretched maid had not caught sight of the offending newspaper, which like the other cuttings, she had managed to sweep out of sight in the nick of time. As for her own jottings, Hilda could not possibly have read them from the doorway. As Florence reluctantly replaced the cap on her fountain pen, she glanced down at the sheet of paper which she had headed 'Discrepancies in the Evidence', the words neatly underlined. She would have to leave it all to one side for now.

CHAPTER NINETEEN

Saturday 20 January 1934
His Majesty's Prison, Armley, Yorkshire

Florence recognised the prison guard who met her at the main entrance as the same one who had conducted her through the labyrinth of Armley Jail on her previous visit to see Ernest Brown. The man seemed to look upon her more kindly on this occasion, and she noticed that when they finally reached the room where Ernest was permitted to receive visitors, he not only pulled out a chair for her to sit on, but accompanied the gesture with something very close to a smile.

She was more nervous this time, more strung up. The first time it had somehow been easier to screw up her courage, because then she had felt that she had to be brave for Freddie's sake. They had not always seen eye to eye – in fact she had often thought her older brother a fool – particularly in his choice of bride, but a brother was a brother and he was the only one she had. On her first visit to the prison, she had been sure of her purpose – she had come to find out the truth for Freddie – this time she was not quite sure for whom she had come. Nor did she know how she would be able to face Brown. How did a man cope with the knowledge that he must die in a day or two – and in a particularly horrible way? What did one say to a man in that position? How did one even look him in the eye?

It was not as if Ernest Brown was a complete stranger, some man who had broken in, or attacked Freddie in the street. She had been aware of Brown for years. An un-regarded figure for the most part, leading horses in a show ring, or busy about the stables, when she had visited her brother's home. A strong, dependable sort of man, of the kind who had always formed the background to lives such as theirs. A man who would have acknowledged her in passing, murmuring her name politely as he touched his cap. Such men could easily become fond of their employer's children. In her own childhood, the family coach driver had often swung herself and Freddie high in the air, led them on their ponies, teased them as he pretended to produce sweets for them from behind their ears. It would have been so easy for Ernest Brown to have maintained an affectionate, yet apparently innocent relationship with baby Diana as she grew, and Freddie never any the wiser.

How much had Freddie actually known, she wondered? He had changed of course, since his marriage. He had always been fond of a drink. It was a family failing – among the men-folk at least – but by the end… staying out at pubs until all hours, and sometimes driving home the worse for drink and spending the night insensible in his car.

A single woman from a good family, Florence had known virtually nothing of relations between husband and wife, until on the recommendation of a woman friend, she had borrowed a book which explained the basic rudiments at least. The book had contained nothing which came anywhere close to explaining why her sister-in-law should be so keen on the activities described in the book, that she had actively sought to perform them with other men as well as with her husband, but that, Florence had decided, was not the point at issue, because when all was said and done, there was no doubt that Dorothy *had* been carrying on with several other men and naturally, if Freddie had found out about it, that must have made him very unhappy.

Unhappy? Mere happiness and unhappiness did not begin to describe what Dorothy had done to them. When Florence allowed herself to feel, when she relaxed her guard and imagined Freddie's body, surrounded by a fiery inferno, Freddie falling to a single shot from a gun… had it only been a single shot? Or had there been others? Had he seen the gun, pleaded for his life? Had he suffered and lingered, as the blood seeped out from his chest? When she allowed those kinds of questions to permeate her consciousness, she felt herself sucked into a void of pain well beyond mere unhappiness. Being unhappy was a picnic spoiled by a rainy day, too many unfilled spaces on a dance card. She saw this same darkness in her father's eyes. His only son gone. Morton & Son without a son to inherit. The knowledge that they would never again hear Freddie's voice, eager and laughing, relaying some hot tip for the races at Wetherby, repeating a funny story he had heard in a pub, or a tale about some old boy he had bumped into at the cattle market. Sometimes, as she proceeded through the day, ordering the meals with Cook, answering her correspondence, politely declining the social invitations which had recommenced, now that Freddie had been dead for several months, she found herself wondering quite how life could possibly go on, just as before.

Then there was Ernest Brown. Unhappy was a poor enough word to encompass his situation too. Unhappy did not come close.

Moreover she was convinced that there was something all wrong about the case. The whole truth had not been told. Though her father had not allowed her to attend the trial itself, she had read pretty much every detail of the evidence in the newspapers, and then Ann Houseman's colourful account as well, and the details sat uneasily, a host of tiny contradictions that did not seem right. Was

it merely that she had misremembered what she had
originally read, or perhaps that the newspapers themselves
had misreported things? Her attempts to sort everything
out in her mind, to compare the different accounts and
get something down on paper, had so far been thwarted
at every attempt. First there had been some trouble over
a tradesman's order and then unexpected callers who had
to be entertained, and now her request for another visit
to Brown himself had been acceded to with unexpected
speed. But there – perhaps there was no point in going
over it all again and again? And yet on the other hand,
surely someone had to try to get to the bottom of it all?

Her chain of thought was interrupted by the opening
of the door at the further end of the room. When Ernest
Brown walked in she was surprised, yet half relieved, to
see that he was unchanged. His 'Miss Morton,' and the
inclination of his head were just as before, and for a split
second, as his eyes met hers, Florence allowed herself to
understand what Dorothy had seen in the man.

'Thank you for agreeing to see me again,' she said.

'Thanks for coming in. It breaks up the day.'

There was a pause. He smiled at her and she found
herself smiling back. He understands, she thought, that
although it's a very terrible situation for him, it is hard
for me too.

'Huddersfield did well in the cup,' he broke the
silence at last. 'Fred would have been pleased. He loved
his football team.'

'Yes,' she said. '6-2 was the final score, I saw it in the paper.'

'Playing like that, they could end up winning it again.'

'Yes, I suppose so.'

What on earth were they doing?' Florence thought, talking about football, when his very life hung in the balance. She would just have to forget polite convention, get to the point and raise the subject that really mattered. 'I saw that your appeal had been turned down,' she said, watching his face carefully.

'Aye, but we're not quite finished yet.'

He sounded surprisingly confident, she thought, for a man whose hopes must now be clinging by a thread.

'Mr Hyams is putting together some statements,' he continued. 'He's a good man, is Mr Hyams. He's stuck by us, right from the off.'

Florence desperately wanted to ask what was in these new statements, and from whom they came, but she was uncertain of the legal etiquette involved and thought that he might not be allowed to tell her, or perhaps that he would not wish to, in front of the guards.

'I expect you know that there's a petition too...' her voice faltered unexpectedly and she didn't complete the sentence.

'So I'm told.'

She looked down at her hands, folded together in her lap, until she had regained mastery of her voice, and was able to look up again and meet his eyes, as she said, 'I have signed it myself.'

A flicker of some indefinable emotion crossed his face, but his voice was perfectly steady as he said, 'Thank you. I appreciate that.'

'I have also written to the Home Secretary.'

'Aye. I believe there's been a lot of letters written.'

'Mr Brown… Ernest… please… If you would only tell the whole truth of what happened…'

A silence hung in the air between them, thick as a woollen blanket. She looked straight into his eyes again and for the first time she fancied that she divined a doubt. He dropped his gaze to the table, an unintended murmur escaping from his lips.

'What did you say? Ernest… Mr Brown, did you say that *you can't?*'

When he remained silent, Florence continued desperately, 'Ernest, I believe you are protecting someone. I am sure you are not telling the whole truth about what happened.'

When he lifted his eyes and faced her again, his features had taken on that strangely neutral, faintly insolent expression, which was both infuriating and yet made her feel a little light headed. 'We've gone over all this before, Miss Morton,' he said. 'With due respect.'

'I could help you,' she said, desperation colouring her tone. 'You forget that I was there, that morning when they were searching for Freddie's body. So was my father. Dorothy was not afraid of you then, was she? She said nothing to any of them then about what terror she and Miss Houseman had suffered the night before – why not, Mr Brown, when the place was crawling with policemen and both of the families and… and all the farm workers too?'

As the prisoner made to get to his feet, both warders instinctively rose from their seats.

'I'm sorry, miss, but you're upsetting the prisoner,' the warder who had escorted her in, now materialised at her side. 'Begging your pardon, but he's not here to be cross examined.'

'No,' she agreed swiftly. 'No, of course not. My apologies, of course.' She hesitated. 'Forgive me, Mr Brown.'

'No offence taken, Miss Morton.'

She noticed that he spoke in the stiff, formal voice which he would always have used for the people who thought themselves his betters. Respectful, yet not entirely sincere. Turning to the warder who had accompanied him from the condemned cell, he said, 'I think I'd like to get back to that game of whist now.'

The warder nodded and as Brown stood up in readiness to leave he said, 'Thank you again for troubling to come in – and thank you for signing the petition and sending the letter and all.'

She stood up too and watched as he walked towards the door in the opposite wall. The door was opened by an unseen hand – someone watching and waiting on the other side of it – and as the warder who had accompanied the condemned man stood aside to let him pass, she realised that once the door had closed behind him, she would not ever see him again. The prison had already swallowed him up and now it would keep him here forever, even his bodily remains consigned to an unmarked burial plot, in the corner of a yard, somewhere unseen to public view.

'Ernest!'

He stopped and turned, framed in the doorway, his face already in the shadow of the corridor beyond.

'You know my address – my father's address – if you should decide to write to me.'

He hesitated, then silently inclined his head, pausing it seemed for one last look at her, before he turned into the corridor and walked away without a word.

CHAPTER TWENTY

Thursday 25 January 1934
Martin's Nest, Yorkshire

Florence was sitting before the drawing room fire when she finally heard her father coming in at in the front door. He was much later than expected, but when he finally entered the room, after the inevitable delay while he divested himself of the winter outer layers, her swift appraisal took in nothing to suggest that the weight of his anxieties had led to a diversion into a local hostelry.

'It took rather longer than expected,' he said, wearily, in answer to her unasked question.

'Poor Daddy,' she said. 'I will ring for Hilda to bring in the tea. Such a horrible day, too.'

They both glanced towards the window panes, obscured by rivulets of wind driven rain.

'I wish you had let me come with you,' she said.

'Nonsense. Court rooms are no place for a respectable woman; whatever would your mother have said? I had your uncle Henry with me. That was enough.'

'And Dorothy? Was she there?'

'Of course.'

'Did you have any conversation with her?'

'There was no need. She was with her father, as usual.'

Florence said nothing. The presence of Dorothy's father, or indeed any one of her other relatives, would have been no reason for not speaking with her back in happier times. Florence wondered what the press and public would have made of it, if they had noticed this complete lack of interaction between these two families, once united by marriage and now driven apart by death.

'Was it very awful? I thought everyone said that completing the inquest was just a formality. Why did it take so long?'

'It shouldn't have taken any time at all. Unfortunately some of the jurors weren't happy. Fellow speaking on their behalf said he didn't see how they could bring in a verdict of murder against Brown, when they hadn't heard the evidence.'

'Oh no.' Florence watched her father anxiously. Surely he had not been subjected to yet another recital of the terrible fire and the blackened body, with its fatal, tell-tale wound? Was there no one who understood what it did to a person, to have to hear it all, over and over again, knowing that the charred flesh had once represented a living, breathing son? Freddie's framed photograph gazed back at her from the mantelpiece: relaxed and smiling, in the year before his marriage, his greyhounds Flash and Joe-bee, held firmly on their leashes, his wide, fashionable cap tipped at a jaunty angle.

At that moment they were interrupted by a tap on the door, followed by the appearance of Hilda and Grace, carrying in the tea. The small table with its starched white cloth was brought before the fire, teapot, milk jug, sugar bowl and tongs, the plates bearing bread and butter, the cake stand with its scones and fruit cake, each in turn dispensed from the big wooden trays. Tea cups tinkling on their saucers, tea plates, napkins, an endless performance, all dragged out to the nth degree, Florence suspected, because the maids were hoping to overhear some titbit or other from Mr Morton's attendance at the inquest; but of course, her father said not another word, until Hilda had made a final, determined assault upon the fire, with the poker, after which both young women had retired from the room and closed the door behind them.

'So what happened?'

'The coroner told the men that they had only to bring in a verdict that was in agreement with the one reached at the assizes. Murder by Ernest Brown.'

'And did that satisfy them?'

'Apparently not. The jury retired to consider the matter and then came back shortly afterwards to say that they did not see how they could come to that verdict.' Her father paused to accept the cup of tea she had poured for him and having set it down at the side of his chair, he helped himself to a piece of fruit cake, ignoring the bread and butter. 'The coroner told them their duty for a second time and this fellow who I suspect was causing all the trouble spoke up again. He said that he did not see that they could be asked to bring in a verdict that they did not all agree with. The coroner asked him what he meant by that and there was some muttering between the men, after which this fellow said that some of them were not satisfied that it had been proved that Brown had murdered Freddie.'

Florence was unable to keep the eagerness out of her voice. 'What happened next?'

'The coroner told them a third time that it was their duty to bring in a verdict in accordance with what had been agreed at the trial. He said they had no power to do anything else.'

'But that's ridiculous! If that is so, then what is the point of holding an inquest at all?'

'The law is the law, my dear.'

'But those men were being asked to deliver a verdict that they did not agree with, as if it were their own.'

Her father said nothing. She waited, but he merely followed the preliminary bite of his cake with another, larger mouthful.

'Did they continue to refuse?'

'No. They retired from the court a second time and when they came back in again, the man appointed foreman – not the fellow who'd been putting up all the objections – recited the verdict.'

'But they were not happy?'

Her father shook his head. What is happy? his expression seemed to say. Florence hesitated, all her doubts, her theories, the contents of the closely written sheets of argument, contained within her dressing table drawer, fluttered around in her mind. For a moment she was determined to say something, but then she recognised his intense weariness. He had lost his only son and come to doubt the paternity of his only grandchild. She understood that it was useless, even to attempt to enlist his aid, in the interests of a man who had cuckolded his darling Freddie.

He broke the silence by announcing: 'At least it's all over.' He picked up his cup and saucer, lifting the cup so as to bring the edge of the china cautiously to his lips, testing the temperature. 'Needs a little more milk,' he said, replacing the cup and using the same hand to reach for the little milk jug.

Not quite all over, Florence thought. She looked across towards the photo in its polished silver frame, but instead of Freddie and his dogs, she saw the tall, dark haired man in prison garb, framed in the doorway as she had seen him last. The execution was set for the first day of February.

CHAPTER TWENTY ONE

Thursday 25 January 1934
Martin's Nest, Yorkshire

The light from the fringed bedside lamp was even duller than usual, Florence noticed. The bulb was probably on the wane. Of course they only used low wattage bulbs in the bedroom, because bedrooms were merely for getting undressed on the hearthrug before climbing into bed, huddled in a nightgown and bed socks, and waiting for the warmth of the hot water bottle and the weight of the bedclothes to take effect. Her late mother had never encouraged the idea of reading in bed, claiming that it was ruinous to the eyes, and refusing to subscribe to Florence's theory that brighter lighting might have made all the difference. Though her mother had been dead for several years now, and Florence was nominally in charge of domestic arrangements, things had not really changed at Martin's Nest.

It would have been harder to make out the words on the sheets she was holding, if she had not written them herself, but as it was, the risk of eye strain was minimised by her familiarity with the contents. The fire in the grate had already diminished to a reddish glow and the hands which emerged from her sensible flannel nightgown were becoming increasingly chilly. The rest of her was warm enough, however, for the covers were pulled well above her chest and her shoulders were swaddled in both a knitted bed-jacket and a shawl, rather as if she were some kind of elderly invalid, she thought.

Though she almost knew them off by heart, she read through the points which she had underlined yet again.

Who was the man that Dolly swam with at Wetherby? Who were her other lovers? Where were these men on the night of the fire?

Dolly said that when Ann got back, they sat in the garden and then made jam, but Ann says that when she got back, she went straight inside and started the jam. Who is correct? Does it matter?

Why didn't Ernest return to the Malt Shovel that night?

Why did no one see Ernest take the shotgun from the cupboard?

Where was Freddie between quarter to nine and half past eleven?

How could Ernest have shot Freddie at half past eleven, if the gun was already back in the cupboard?

If Dolly saw Ernest putting the white handled knife back in the drawer, why was it found in a wheelbarrow in the yard the next morning?

Dolly and Ann say that they heard nothing moving on the drive until Freddie freewheeled the Chrysler down it at half past eleven, but Ernest says that by then he had already freewheeled the Essex down to the garage – why didn't they hear that? (NB. Someone must have moved the Essex at some point, because it was found burned out in the garage.)

No man should be found guilty while there is a reasonable doubt, she thought, yet here there were doubts aplenty, and Ernest Brown had never the less been condemned to die. Had no one else observed all these strange discrepancies? Was there no one else who thought that they mattered? Surely it was not too late to do something, if she only knew what.

It was useless writing to the newspapers, who were all set dead against Ernest Brown since the verdict, and anyway she knew that to publically associate herself with the campaign to save him would only attract more notoriety and she was not sure how much more of it her poor father could stand. When she had tentatively attempted to raise some of her doubts with him that night after supper, he had made it perfectly clear that he considered the matter closed and just wanted to be left in peace.

She knew that the last word rested with the Home Secretary, because that was the person to whom the petition entreating mercy for Ernest Brown had been addressed, but she had written to the Home Secretary once already, and though almost a week had passed, she had yet to receive a reply. Then she remembered what Ernest had said about Mr Hyams. Perhaps even now the young solicitor from Huddersfield was putting together the file of evidence which would save his client's neck.

Well… perhaps not precisely now, since it was past eleven o'clock at night. She shuffled her sheets of paper together and placed them in a neat little pile on the bedside table, before extending her hand a little further until her outstretched fingers encountered the switch on the base of her bedside lamp, which she pressed down to extinguish the light. Now there was just the faint glow from the fireplace and the occasional sound of one coal shifting against another. She slid beneath the bedclothes and shut her eyes, but sleep eluded her, just as it had for far too many nights before.

CHAPTER TWENTY TWO

Friday 26 January 1934
The Home Office, Whitehall, London

Charles Featherstone stood silently before the Sir John Gilmour's desk, trying to ignore the pain from his chilblains, while the Home Secretary seemed to take an age to read and initial the papers before him, and then to take what seemed like another age to fussily re-order them on the treasury tag, fold the manila cover of the file back together, then pass it up to Featherstone in a movement to which they were both so accustomed that their two hands might have been part of a single machine.

'Anything else, Featherstone?'

'One more thing, Sir John. A letter in regard to the Brown case.'

The Home Secretary emitted a sound which was somewhere between a snort and a sigh. Charles Featherstone was well aware of the amount of time which had already been taken up with matters pertaining to this particular prisoner. Only a couple of days ago there had been a stay of execution, thanks to the arrival of a letter from some meddlesome fellow in Huddersfield, claiming that Ernest Brown's grandfather had ended his days in an asylum and suggesting that insanity ran in his family. Thanks to there having been some suggestion during the trial, that the man had behaved in a thoroughly irrational manner on the night of the murder, it had been deemed necessary to bring in a psychiatrist to examine Brown, in addition to which, the doctor who had treated his family ever since he was a boy had also been approached for information, but neither had been able to report anything which remotely implied that the fellow should escape the hangman on the grounds that he was a lunatic, and as a result, his date with the execution chamber had now been slated for 6 February. This in turn had sparked a further flurry of protest, mostly in the form of letters to the newspapers, or else direct to the Home Office, arguing that it was disgraceful to torment a man by constantly promising him death, but then postponing it.

'Another one?' Sir John said, without bothering to disguise the weariness in his tone. 'I thought you had Beach dealing with all of those?'

'This one is slightly different, sir. In the first place it is addressed to you personally, but the really unusual aspect is that the letter appears to have been written by the sister of the deceased in the case.' A quizzical look from his boss encouraged him to continue. 'The letter comes from a Miss Florence Morton, sir, and she appears to be suggesting that the man Brown is innocent.'

'Are you sure that it's genuine, Featherstone? Did the dead man even have a sister? You know what some of these cranks and fraudsters are like.'

'The letter arrived several days ago, sir, and I have already taken the liberty of making some enquiries. So far as it has been possible for me to ascertain, the letter does indeed emanate from the victim's sister.'

'How very odd. The relatives are generally at the forefront in baying for the guilty party's blood. Is she a crank herself – or an abolitionist perhaps?'

'The young woman writes in a perfectly rational manner, and she makes no objection to hanging per se, merely to hanging what she perceives as an innocent man. If I may suggest, Sir John, irrespective of the contents, a personal reply would appear indicated, given her very close association with the case.'

'Quite so. Very well, hand it over. Let's see what Miss Morton has to say.'

Featherstone shifted his weight from one foot to the other, while the Home Secretary began to read.

'Are we still getting many letters of protest about this one?' Gilmour asked, without looking up.

'Quite a few. The usual complement who claim to have received communications from the spirit world or via dreams, the blue crayon and completely dotty brigade obviously, a handful ratting on neighbours who could not possibly have been anywhere near the scene of the crime at the right time, and a significant number who wish to inform you that the outcome has shaken their confidence in British justice.'

'Indeed. I get the impression that the man Brown must have a lot of friends and supporters, who are committed to doing some rabble rousing in the immediate locality. There were some very unpleasant scenes outside the court, after the verdict, if I remember correctly.'

'A great many of the letters we are receiving do not appear to come from the immediate area, or indeed from the class of person to which Brown and his friends presumably belong, sir.'

'Really?' The Home Secretary's response was half hearted. He was still engrossed in the letter. '*Never any sign at all that my sister-in-law was afraid of Brown, or indeed anyone else…*' he read aloud. 'This is quite interesting… *after receiving the telephone call from Miss Houseman, telling us that there had been a fire, my father and I drove straight to Saxton Grange. When our car turned into the drive at about half past nine that morning, we immediately came upon Dorothy, standing out on the drive, talking to Ernest Brown, and not apparently in the least afraid of him. Afterwards she was going about telling everyone that he had been perfectly splendid, getting the horses out. PC Broadhead was there at the time, and if Dorothy had been so afraid of him, why did she not simply get him arrested?'* Gilmour looked up, apparently expecting some kind of comment.

'It would appear to be a reasonable point, sir.'

'The first thing Dorothy said to myself and my father was, "Isn't it awful? But you know, it's all his own fault. I warned him repeatedly about coming home in that condition, running the car into the garage and falling asleep. I expect it was a cigarette which caused it. I kept on telling him something like this would happen and now it has. There is nothing left of him at all – nothing." Later on Dorothy and I went into the house together. My father stayed outside, talking to Dorothy's father, who had also arrived. When we entered the drawing room, Dorothy walked across and looked at one of Freddie's photographs, which was in a frame on the piano. Then she said, "Everyone thinks that the child looks like him, but there is nothing left of him, nothing." During all the time that we were together that morning, she said nothing at all in accusation against Ernest Brown, although there was ample opportunity. Tell me, wasn't that point raised at the original trial?'

'I believe it was suggested at one point, that Mrs Morton had not initially indicated her suspicions of Brown to the police.'

'And was Miss Morton called as a witness? Ahh…
no… she wasn't. She says as much here. According to
Miss Morton's letter then, the widow doesn't start telling
people that she is afraid of the man Brown until after it
was realised that her husband had been murdered. Here
it is… *When my father and I arrived at Saxton Grange to
support Dorothy, on the day that the inquest opened, she
had changed her attitude to Brown entirely, and instead
of telling people that he had been positively heroic on the
night of the fire, she tried to tell me that she did not want to
go to the inquest, as Ernest Brown would be there, and she
was afraid of what he might do to her. I was bewildered by
this change of heart, and in any case, Brown was in police
custody at the time… Having learned more of my brother's
married life, I now believe that Dorothy never loved him…
when he was buried in Saxton Church, it was a hole-in-
the-corner affair, and when the vicar asked Freddie's age
for the burial register, Dorothy said, "Oh put about thirty."*
The Home Secretary glanced up, eyebrows expressively
raised.

'Hmm – not much love lost between Miss Morton
and her sister-in-law, is there? Possible motive for the
letter, could be jealousy. These spinsters can become
extremely jealous of other women – especially those
who are glamorous and have married well. Young women
can sometimes get fixated on their brothers, in a quite
unhealthy way, or so I've heard. Do you know anything
about that sort of business, Featherstone?'

'I cannot say that I do, sir.'

'Ahh... here it comes... *it was not pointed out to the jury that my sister-in-law benefitted under my brother's will, and has inherited his entire estate, worth some £18,700.* Well there we are.' Gilmour placed the letter flat on the desk before him and tapped the relevant sentence with a fingertip. 'Jealousy, Featherstone, what did I tell you? No doubt the sister and her father are upset that the farm and all the assets are passing out of the family's hands.'

'Circumstances which are likely to cause a great deal of resentment.' The civil servant nodded, while trying to blot out the burning sensations, which continued to emanate from his chilblains.

'Draft a letter for me will you, thanking the young woman for her trouble in writing, usual expressions of sympathy of course, every confidence in the verdict, all the points she raised thoroughly gone into at the trial and appeal and so on, and now the law must take its course. You know the line to take.'

'Yes, sir. Of course.' Featherstone waited politely, until the Home Secretary picked up the letter and handed it back to him. It would have been presumptuous to merely lean across and retrieve it from the desk himself.

'I suppose the young woman has now developed some sort of crush on the man Brown.' Gilmour shook his head. 'These girls do get the strangest fancies, and of course he had initially been involved in some sort of affair with Mrs Morton, so I suppose there must be something about him which women find attractive. Married too, wasn't he?'

'A widower, sir. I believe his wife had not been dead very long at the time of the Morton murder.'

'I see... What happened to the wife, do you know? The local police looked into all that, I suppose?'

'Oh yes, Sir John. It was confirmed that she had died of natural causes.'

'Is Miss Morton an attractive girl, I wonder? One tends to imagine a letter like this coming from a Plain Jane.'

'I have no idea, sir,' said Featherstone, who had never found any girls remotely attractive.

'Very well,' the Home Secretary said, adopting a brisker tone. 'Is that the last of it for now?'

'Yes sir, nothing else needing your immediate attention at the moment.'

'Thank goodness for that. I have to get away for five thirty, or we will never make the dinner at the Mansion House.'

CHAPTER TWENTY THREE

Monday 29 January 1934
The Home Office, Whitehall, London

There was a bright fire burning in the grate of Sir John Gilmour's office, but the young solicitor from Huddersfield was given scant opportunity to warm himself, for after extending a hand, accompanied by a greeting, Sir John announced: 'I don't have very much time, Mr Hyams, so I need you to make this as brief as possible. Please do take a seat.'

'Yes, sir. Of course. It's very good of you to see me at such short notice.' Hyams perched on the edge of the chair which had been indicated, shuffled in his briefcase and brought out the neatly clipped sheaf of statements that he had gathered together. An interview with the Home Secretary had been almost more than he had dared to hope for. 'If you would be so good as to look at these…' he began.

He got no further. Sir John made an impatient gesture with his hand, which stated more clearly than words that he did not have time to scrutinise several sheets of double spaced foolscap. 'Summarise, Mr Hyams. Summarise. Perhaps you should begin by telling me why you have left it so late in the day to make this approach on behalf of your client?'

Hyams obediently retracted the hand that held the statements. 'I do realise that it is very late in the day,' he said apologetically. 'You see I have been trying to trace the whereabouts of a young woman who used to work at Saxton Grange – a Miss Kathleen Holmes – who it is thought could shed more light on the relationship between my client and Mrs Morton.'

'Are you telling me that after all this time, the police have failed to trace one of the servants who might have been a witness to the events that night?'

'No, sir. Miss Holmes left the Morton's employment in early July, in order to take up a position elsewhere. Unfortunately my client recalls only that it was somewhere in the south of the country. However, she had been employed at Saxton Grange throughout the period during which Ernest Brown was ahem… paying attentions to Mrs Morton, and so she was fully aware of the footing on which their relationship stood.'

'But she was not actually working for the Mortons at the time of the murder?'

'No, and I regret to say that we have been unable to track her down in her new employment.'

'But this was the cause of the delay? Very well then, let us turn to this new evidence which you say you do have. Let's begin by having the reasons why this evidence was not heard at Brown's original trial, or indeed his appeal.'

'Mr Streatfield did not consider the evidence admissible at the trial or at the appeal.'

'Why not?'

'I am not entirely clear on the point, sir.'

'And of course, you are a provincial solicitor, while Mr Streatfield is a King's Counsel.'

'Precisely.' Hyams readily swallowed the insult. The important thing was the opportunity he had secured for his client.

'So what is this important testimony, which was not heard?'

'At the trial, sir, Mrs Dorothy Morton, wife of the deceased…'

'I know who Mrs Morton is.'

'Yes sir, quite so. Mrs Morton stated in her sworn evidence that when Brown left her husband's employment in June, it was because of a dispute concerning a lawn mower. Essentially she claimed that he left in a hasty, ill-considered way, having lost his temper, and then thought better of the decision almost immediately and demanded to be reinstated. According to Mrs Morton, Brown initially wrote to her, asking for his job back, and when that met with a negative response, she claims that he returned to the farm and threatened her with violence, if she did not persuade her husband to reinstate him.

'Brown tells a completely different story. He claims that he had decided to leave because he had grown tired of working at Saxton Grange and intended to obtain alternative employment, closer to his daughter and his family. According to Ernest Brown, two days after he left, while he was staying at his mother's home in Huddersfield, he received a long letter from Mrs Morton, begging him to return, protesting her great affection for him and in particular saying that their child – the baby girl which had been born the previous year – was missing him. The child, she said, kept asking where "Brownie" was.

'Brown was at home when this letter from Mrs Morton arrived and he showed it to his mother, and to his brother-in-law, Charles Wilson, who happened to be there at the time. Both of them read the letter and are prepared to swear to the gist of the contents. I have their statements with me here. Brown also discussed the arrival of the letter with a couple of his friends in the pub that evening, because he was still trying to decide whether or not to return to Saxton Grange. Brown apparently showed them the envelope, which he had been carrying in his jacket pocket and though he did not offer to show them the letter itself, he gave them an idea of what Mrs Morton had written. They too are prepared to swear to this conversation having taken place. I have their statements too.' Mr Hyams tapped a forefinger on the sheets lying in his lap, as if to emphasise their contents.

'As a result of the letter, ' he continued, 'Brown decided to return to Saxton Grange, travelling there by bus the following day, but in the meantime Mrs Morton had sent a further letter, again imploring him to return: a letter which of course then lay unopened at the home of Brown's mother. When Mrs Morton discovered that this letter must have arrived after Brown's departure that morning, she became extremely concerned about the possibility that it might fall into the wrong hands and she drove Brown all the way back to Huddersfield, in order to retrieve this second missive. Brown's mother and sister were there when Brown arrived in Mrs Morton's motor car, and have given statements to the effect that they saw Mrs Morton sitting outside in the car, waiting while Brown came inside the house to collect Mrs Morton's second letter. No one of course knows what the contents of this second letter were, but they can no doubt be inferred by Mrs Morton's enthusiasm to have it back.'

'And what is supposed to have happened to these letters?'

'Mrs Morton asked to have them back and Brown gave them to her. She told Brown that she did not wish there to be any chance of the letters falling into her husband's hands, and that she therefore intended to burn them, which presumably she did.'

'How convenient.'

Mr Hyams affected not to notice the Home Secretary's tone. 'This does prove that Mrs Morton lied both in regard to her relationship with Brown and about the circumstances surrounding his return to the Morton household in June.'

'With respect, Mr Hyams, I do not see that it does. In such cases it is hardly unusual for the family and friends of the accused to concoct extenuating evidence, which cannot of course be proved, one way or the other. Besides which, I do not see that what happened in June, has any great bearing on what happened in September. Irrespective of the precise relationship between Mrs Morton and the man Brown in early summer, the jury and the court of appeal concluded that it was Brown who shot her husband dead in early autumn.'

Mr Hyams opened his mouth to speak, but the Home Secretary was already getting to his feet and extending his hand. 'Thank you for coming to see me, Mr Hyams. I know that your journey has been a long one, and your efforts on the part of your client do you great credit, but I am afraid that there is really nothing more that can be done.'

CHAPTER TWENTY FOUR

Sunday 4 February 1934
His Majesty's Prison, Armley, Yorkshire

'I don't envy you your job these last few weeks,' Albert Henshaw swilled down the last of his tea, in readiness to resume his shift.

'Only a day and a bit, now.' Joe Fazackerley said. 'I've not done duty in the condemned cell before and I don't mind telling you, I hope I don't have to do it again.'

'They say in the paper as there's nine thousand signatures on that petition now. Not that it will change their minds.' Albert maintained a neutral tone. He remained curious about the bloke Brown, and the way his case seemed to generate doubts in a way which most convicted felons did not. Yet at the same time he knew that a man ought not to doubt the system. If it reached the chief warder's ears that Joe Fazackerley appeared to have gone soft, he would probably be removed from that particular duty. The chaplain was one thing. The prison warders themselves, another.

'Nothing will change now,' Fazackerley agreed, quietly.

The minute hand of the big wall clock jerked on another minute, reaching the quarter hour and thereby marking the end of their tea break. As Joe Fazackerley walked steadily back towards the condemned cell, his thoughts turned to the little newsagent's shop which had recently gone up for sale at the end of his street. He had never seen himself as a shopkeeper, but perhaps it was time to think about a change. Elsie would be able to give him a hand in there, now that the youngest was off her hands, during school hours at least. They had enough put by in the Leeds and Holbeck Building Society to put up a deposit, and the place always appeared to do a brisk enough trade, situated as it was, right close to the tram stop.

As he approached the cell door, Eddie Bottomley who was on duty outside, rose to unlock it for him and as he stepped inside, George Tyler, his relief, rose to greet him, putting on his cap and straightening his collar as he did so, before exchanging farewells with the other warder, Harry Gregory, and the prisoner himself.

'Good night, Ernest.'

They all called him Ernest. A degree of familiarity was permitted between this particular prisoner and the small group of men who sat with him, always two at a time. It was their job to keep him calm. You didn't want a prisoner in his situation to start getting upset or rattled, screaming or shouting out, or throwing a fit and getting violent. Trouble like that could easily spread. There was always a faint air of tension throughout the rest of the prison, when they had a man awaiting execution.

In this case the whole thing had dragged on for far too long already. The date had been set back twice now, firstly for the appeal and then because there had been a letter from some doctor in Huddersfield, suggesting that there was insanity in Brown's family; though of course that had all turned out to be something of nothing. Fazackerley unconsciously shook his head. They would spare the barmy ones, however many lives they had taken, but sometimes hanged the innocent ones. No, he did not think that, not really. Though assailed by creeping doubts over Brown's conviction, you had to believe that the jury had got it right. It was a good system, the finest in the world.

It must be slow torture for the condemned man, he thought, all this uncertainty over exactly when it would happen, though Brown had borne it well.

'It's because he still thinks that he's going to get off,' Harry Gregory had said, one morning, as they fetched their bicycles from the shed, ready to ride home at the conclusion of a shift. He had followed the remark up with an abrupt bark of laughter, adding: 'And that *is* barmy.'

Pulling himself firmly back into the present, Joe said, 'Do you fancy another game of dominoes, Ernest, or are you about ready to turn in for the night?'

The prisoner hesitated. He was sitting on the side of his bed, where he had previously been chatting with Tyler and Gregory. He wasn't a big talker, but when he had something to say, it had generally been worth listening to. He was well informed, for a man of his class, and forthright with his opinions. You learned a lot about a man, sitting with him, hour after hour, for six long weeks. Though raised in a town, he loved the countryside. There wasn't much he didn't know about the welfare and husbandry of horses, but he was also well-up on the repair and maintenance of motor vehicles. He had spoken affectionately of his relations and appeared to have a very wide circle of friends. 'Meeting him in the pub, you wouldn't have had him down as a murderer,' Harry Gregory had once remarked.

He was easy to like, that was the trouble. He told them that he'd always had a quick temper, but there hadn't been much sign of that in here. By and large he had given them no trouble, aside from occasionally being a bit cheeky, while on remand. He liked a laugh and a joke and he'd told them one or two good stories, these last few weeks, retaining his sense of humour, even in this cheerless place.

The warders had been curious of course, about the crime itself, but they were under strict instructions not to ask for any details, and Ernest had volunteered none, explaining nothing, but simply acting as if he was confident of a reprieve. Surely now, Joe thought, he must realise that it wasn't going to come? The chaplain had taken to visiting every day, and Ernest had been reading his Bible as Reverend Hadfield had advised him to. Apparently Ernest had attended the Mission Hall in Huddersfield as a lad, which had proved a point of connection between them, for Joe Fazackerley too had been raised a Methodist, and they had exchanged memories of favourite hymns together. Aye, there was none as could sing out like a Methodist. (Harry Gregory, a Baptist himself, had begged to disagree.)

'I want to get word to Miss Morton.' The prisoner's words came unexpectedly, startling Joe out of his reverie.

'How do you mean, Ernest?' Harry Gregory asked.

'I'd like to see her – as soon as possible.'

'But it's ten o'clock at night.'

'I know. I meant tomorrow. I'd like to get word to her to come in and see me tomorrow.'

Joe hesitated, glancing at Gregory. 'We won't be able to do anything now Ernest. Shifts have changed and there will be no one in the office until the morning. I daresay they could send word then, but…'

Harry helped him out: 'There's no guarantee that she would get the message. She might not be at home and…'

'And time's running short,' Ernest finished for him.

'Are you sure that she would want to come?' Joe asked, quietly. 'It's a big thing, for a young woman to come into the jail like that.'

'She will come. She's asked me for the truth and I want to give it to her.'

'Ernest – what exactly do you mean? Are you saying that you haven't told the whole truth until now?' Joe's tone was cautious. They were not to upset the prisoner, or ask him probing questions, but on the other hand, if he was minded to make a clean breast of it, a final confession before witnesses, it would put a lot of minds at rest and stifle all these do-gooders who'd been hanging about near the prison gates, waving placards and shouting after officers, when they arrived for work or left for home.

'I want to tell Miss Morton what really happened. She's a good sort and she deserves to know. And her father too. Loves his horses does Mr Morton. I've known him since I were only a lad myself. He often had a kind word for me at shows, and it was him as recommended me to work for Fred in the first place. I saw the way he looked at me, when he thought it was me as had killed his son. It upset me at the time but I thought I must keep quiet, you see.'

'Only now you've changed your mind?'

'I have. But it's to Miss Morton I want to tell what really happened.'

'Ernest,' Joe leaned forward in his chair. 'A request like this is very unusual, especially with Miss Morton not being a member of your family and all. It would have to go through the governor and even if he agreed to it, we may not be able to get Miss Morton here in time.' He paused. Brown was watching him, taking in and weighing up what he said. Joe abruptly recalled those descriptions which the two women had given of him at the trial, a man who had supposedly looked 'wild' and 'mad'. Yet here was this same man facing imminent death, and Joe thought that he had seldom seen a man who looked more calm and resolute. A man who having made up his mind to do something, now intended to see it through.

'If you were to tell us what it is that you want to tell Miss Morton, and we were able to pass this on to the governor tomorrow morning, that might help persuade him to send for Miss Morton.'

The man on the bunk hesitated. After an almost unbearably long pause, he drew in a breath and said, 'Very well. I'll tell you what really happened.'

CHAPTER TWENTY FIVE

Monday 5 February 1934
His Majesty's Prison, Armley, Yorkshire

John Wilton, recently promoted to prison governor's secretary, sat at his desk in the corner of the most comfortable room in Armley Jail and watched as the prisoner and his guards came marching through the doorway. He had never seen Ernest Brown in the flesh and like the majority of the population of Yorkshire and beyond, entertained a certain amount of curiosity about the man. In Wilton's case the level of curiosity had been considerably elevated by the conversation which he had overheard between his gaffer and Brown's guards, Fazackerly and Gregory, just half an hour earlier.

After spending almost three months on remand, followed by another six weeks in the condemned cell, being ushered into the governor's office must be akin to entering another world, Wilton thought. The echoing corridors, clanging iron gates, perpetual clatter of keys and distant voices raised against the general clamour, all of which made up the prisoners' world, abruptly transformed into an oasis of leather chairs (not that the prisoner would be invited to sit down of course) and polished wooden desks, a clear glass, unbarred window, and a carpet, patterned in red and black, which deadened the sound of Ernest's feet, and those of his inevitable escort, the familiar shapes of Bottomley and Jordan, his minders for the day shift.

'Now then, Brown.' The governor's voice was firm but not unkind. 'This story which you told the officers, in your cell last night – can you explain to me why you have withheld it until now?'

It was clearly not the question which he had been anticipating, and for a moment Ernest Brown hesitated, emitting no more than a small choking sound, the product of a dry throat.

'It is quite different to the story you have been telling all along, isn't it?' coaxed the governor. 'It's not at all the same as the story which you told, on oath, in court.'

'No sir.' Now that the man had found his voice it came out strongly.

'Which of these stories is correct? The one you told on oath, after placing your hand on the Holy Bible, or the one you are telling us now, when you have taken no oath at all to tell the truth?'

'The one that I'm telling now is the truth.'

'Address the governor as "sir".' Bert Jordan issued a swift reminder.

'The one that I am telling now, sir.'

'Would you be willing to tell this new story after taking such an oath? Bearing in mind that your time on earth now is liable to be short? That having stood before an earthly court, you will soon be standing before the court of Heaven?'

'I am not afraid to stand before the court of Heaven, sir, for I believe they will give me fairer judgement there than I have had on earth.' Ernest held his head erect and looked the man behind the desk right in the eyes. 'I am perfectly willing to swear on the Bible, the life of my daughter, or anything else you care to suggest, that the story I told last night is the true one.'

'So, let us return to the original question. Can you explain why you have waited until now to tell this story? You realise that it is probably too late to save yourself?'

'I do, sir.'

'Then why are you telling this new story now?'

'I have been thinking of Miss Morton, sir. She asked me to tell her the truth and last night, I finally decided that I should. Mr Fazackerley and Mr Gregory told me that if I explained the whole circumstances to them, it might make you more favourably inclined to asking Miss Morton to come and visit, so that I can explain it all to her in person.'

'So you have come up with this story in order to gain a last visit from Miss Morton?'

'No, sir.' Ernest refused to be riled. 'I have decided to tell Miss Morton the truth. I've kept silent until now, but in doing so, I can see that I have wronged Miss Morton. I don't want to die with a lie on my conscience and her not knowing how her brother met his end. She desired to have the truth and I have decided to give it to her.'

'Let us return to our starting point. I understand what you say about Miss Morton, but for goodness sake, man, you have been under sentence of death for these past six weeks. Surely you did not want to die for a crime which you say you did not commit?'

'But I did not believe that I was going to die, sir.'

There was a mulish note in the prisoner's voice, which Wilton could tell was exasperating the governor.

'How can you possibly say that? You stood in court and were sentenced, were you not? You attended your appeal and heard it turned down. You have known for weeks now that you were to face execution. How could you have believed otherwise?'

'I believed British justice to be the finest in the world. That's what everyone says, isn't it? An innocent man has nothing to fear. I didn't believe they could find me guilty.' Wilton detected an unmistakable hint of bitterness, bordering on recrimination, in the man's tone.

The governor inhaled deeply, but before he could respond, the prisoner continued, 'Beyond reasonable doubt, it's supposed to be, sir. How could they find me guilty, when I hadn't committed the crime? And even when the jury said I was guilty, I thought it would be looked at. I thought someone higher up would look into it and see that I was an innocent man.'

'But you now admit that you told the court lies.'

'It shouldn't matter what you say – lies or not – if you're innocent then you're innocent,' Ernest said stubbornly.

'It is highly irregular, Brown, and I warn you now that I can make no promises, but I will have some sheets of foolscap sent to your cell and I want you to write down the story that you told Fazackerley and Gregory last night, and that they in turn have told me this morning. It is just faintly possible, that some "higher-ups" as you put it, may be willing to consider what you have to say. I assume that you are prepared to put this story down on paper?'

'Yes sir, of course.'

'Very well then. You will need to make a quick job of it. Time is pressing. See what you can do, and when it is finished,' the governor's glance embraced Bottomley and Jordan, both standing silent and impassive to either side of their charge, 'I want it brought to me immediately. It goes without saying that none of this is to be discussed beyond the walls of this office and of Brown's quarters.'

'Yes sir.'

After chorusing their agreement, the warders prepared to escort Brown out of the room, but though the governor had glanced away, his attention momentarily distracted by a gust of wind which flung a handful of hailstones against the window, Wilton saw that the groom from Huddersfield had not quite finished.

'Begging your pardon, sir, but what about Miss Morton?'

From his corner, Wilton noted that while Brown's words were always polite, his tone never became craven or subservient.

The governor turned back to find the prisoner still standing in the same position as before. 'I have noted your request regarding Miss Morton.'

'Thank you, sir.' Only now was Brown prepared to follow the lead from his guards, and turning on his heel, he marched smartly from the room.

It had hardly been necessary to reiterate the element of secrecy, Wilton thought. The entire prison had been placed in lockdown for the duration of Brown's outing to the governor's office, in order to ensure that none of the other inmates should be aware that there was anything unusual going on. Now that the trio were on their way back to Brown's normal quarters and the door had closed behind them, the governor turned his attention to his secretary.

'Wilton, kindly organise the necessary writing materials to be taken down to the condemned cell immediately. Then get the Home Secretary on the telephone.'

'Sir John Gilmour, sir?'

'Of course Sir John Gilmour. The holder of the office hasn't changed since yesterday evening, has it?'

'No sir. Of course not. And what about Miss Morton, sir?'

'What about Miss Morton?'

'Do you wish me to attempt to communicate with the lady, sir? We have her address – and possibly her telephone number – in the file.'

'Certainly not. Not only would it be highly irregular, but we simply cannot start a hare running. There has been quite enough fuss and agitation about this particular case already.'

Prisoners were supplied with a limited amount of prison notepaper for their letters, but that would clearly be inadequate for the matter in hand. Deciding that the fastest way to get the sheets of foolscap down to Brown would be to take them from his own supply of stationery and send them with Partridge, the minion who occupied a desk just outside the governor's door, Wilton went immediately to the large cupboard which stood in an alcove adjacent to his desk, and began to count out some sheets from his stock. In prison, everything was counted and recorded. He decided that four, which allowed for eight sides of writing, would be more than enough. Emerging from behind the cupboard door, he saw that the governor, generally very much a stranger to idleness, was sitting at his desk with folded hands, staring at the panels of the door through which Ernest Brown and his guards had recently departed, much as if he was mentally following them on their long walk back to Brown's quarters.

Wilton decided to be bold. 'What do you make of it, sir? This new story that Brown is telling?'

'I don't know, Wilton. Quite frankly, I don't know. However, if it is something which may make a difference to his case, then naturally it is my duty to pursue the matter.'

'Naturally, sir.'

CHAPTER TWENTY SIX

Monday 5 February 1934
The Home Office, Whitehall, London

'So come on Featherstone, old chap. You must know what's going on.'

'It's confidential.'

Seeing that the two men were alone, James Hedley-Bruce decided that it was safe to give his colleague a friendly nudge, while saying, 'Dear boy, it's always confidential.' He knew perfectly well that Featherstone wouldn't hold out on him – he never did. Besides which, even in his own much less senior capacity, he was aware of one or two of the details, because Featherstone had already asked him to make a couple of telephone calls.

Charles Featherstone glanced over his shoulder conspiratorially – an entirely unnecessary measure in the otherwise deserted office – and said, 'It's the man Ernest Brown. Under sentence of death at Leeds and supposed to hang tomorrow morning.'

'I guessed as much.'

'There's been a telephone call from the prison governor. Apparently this Brown chap made a clean breast of things to the prison warders last night.'

'I've heard that a lot of them do that at the end. So if he's admitted it at last, why all the fuss?'

'You don't understand. Brown isn't confessing, apparently he has named someone else.'

'But wasn't he pleading not guilty all along?'

'Yes, but apparently this new story – well – the prison governor seems to think that there might be something in it.'

'The "something" presumably being that Brown didn't do it after all, because he can prove that somebody else did?'

'Apparently so.'

'Bit late for a last ditch appeal.'

'There can't be another appeal. There's no legal precedent for it. The only possibility now would be a Royal Pardon.'

'Involving the King himself.'

'His Majesty will always follow whatever the Home Sec recommends in matters like these.'

'And what does Sir John think about it all?'

Featherstone shrugged. 'It's a hot potato. You can't win with the public, when it comes to executions.'

'And is this fellow Brown telling the truth, do you think?'

'Who knows? A man of that type would say anything to save his own skin, I would imagine.'

'Well so would I!'

'What? Say anything?'

'In that situation? Of course I would. The fellow's probably lying through his teeth. So what's the old man going to do about it?'

'He's got the prison governor to catch the train down to London, bringing this new confession with him.'

'The prison governor himself eh?' Hedley-Brown drew in a breath through pursed lips, making the air whistle as it crossed his lower teeth.

'The prison governor himself,' Featherstone repeated. He wished that Hedley-Bruce was not given to such extravagant gestures as whistling through his teeth. An unattractive sort of activity in an otherwise very attractive young man. 'In the meantime the Home Sec is assembling some of the original team from the trial to meet the DPP and discuss it. This is very hush hush,' he added.

'Of course. So that's why he wanted me to get old Paley Scott on the blower this morning.'

'Exactly so. The Home Sec's reasoning is that the original judge and prosecuting counsel will know enough about the case to tell whether or not there's anything in what the fellow is saying now.'

'Not the defence barristers?'

'Not the defence barristers. They have an interest you see. It would put them in an impossible situation, given that they were originally being paid to get the chap off.'

Hedley-Bruce considered this for a moment and thought of pointing out that the same must also be true of the prosecuting barristers, since they had been paid to get the man convicted in the first place, but he decided against, saying instead, 'Well he was out of luck with Travers Humphreys, because he's presiding over a trial in Leicester.'

'But luckily the two counsel and the DPP are available and they are due to arrive here at around midday or just after.'

'And will the Home Sec be participating himself?'

'No. Sir John doesn't feel that he is as fully briefed on the case as the legal chappies – and anyway, he has a pretty full diary today. You are to make the arrangements for luncheon by the way. Just for the DPP and the two barristers.'

'Not for the prison governor?'

'Not for the prison governor. He won't be party to the discussion.'

'Just the errand boy,' murmured the younger man. He liked old Featherstone, but he did wish the chap wouldn't keep repeating things – talk about Little Sir Echo. He sometimes wondered whether Featherstone had been so long in the service that he had become completely expert in never allowing the mask to slip, or whether he just habitually accepted the official line. Perhaps it never occurred to him that even if not fully conversant with the ins and outs of the case, Sir John must surely know a lot more about it than the average man in the street, and moreover represented – on the face of it at least – a completely neutral perspective. He's ducking it, Hedley-Bruce thought. And in his place, I might just do the same. It was an awful responsibility, having to decide whether a man was going to live or going to die.

CHAPTER TWENTY SEVEN

Monday 5 February 1934
Martin's Nest, Holywell Green, Yorkshire

'For goodness sake, Miss Florence, have you got ants in your pants?' Nanny's unseemly imprecation against fidgeting came unbidden into her head, as Florence shifted the cushions and tried to settle to reading the morning paper. The expression had invariably conjured up such a horrid mental image, that it had always made poor Florence want to wriggle all the more.

Her early childhood had been similarly darkened by such exclamations as: 'This drawer looks as if a bunch of rattle snakes has been through it,' and more terrifying still, 'If you don't leave that nose alone, the Bogey Man will come for you tonight.'

The Bogey Man.

Lately her nights had been haunted by far worse – that was when she had managed to get off to sleep at all. When she looked at herself in the dressing table mirror, she could see tell-tale dark shadows beneath her eyes. She must not think of her childhood, because whereas at one time the thought of Freddie tormenting her, as he had so often done, could still make her hot with indignation (he had been Nanny's favourite and always got away with murder) now it just made her want to cry. Poor silly, besotted Freddie, who had even pretended to be older than he was, in order to impress Dorothy Middlemost. Oh Freddie, Freddie, why ever were you such a fool as to marry her?

But of course, Florence thought, everyone – herself included – had initially fallen under Dolly's spell. She was so handsome, so lively. That sharp wit and such energy, with a willingness to throw herself into anything and everything, whether it be organising a tea party for war veterans, or a family game of charades at Christmas. 'You should see her out hunting,' Freddie had once told his sister. 'She's absolutely fearless.'

Florence had long ago admitted to herself that she too had, at one time, been in complete awe of her sister-in-law. Dolly was so confident and clever; but gradually she had begun to sense, rather than see, another side to Dolly. There was something steely at her core. A hard, determined streak which meant that Dolly was going to get what she wanted, even if it meant squashing flat the hopes and aspirations of everyone else, or bending the will of others to her own.

Florence had once remarked to her father that, 'If Brown did shoot Freddie, then it was only because Dolly told him to.'

'Don't be silly,' her father had said gravely.

That had been in the early days, when she and her father could still bring themselves to speak to one another of the tragedy. Later she had begun to avoid the subject and in the past few days she had stopped speaking of it altogether, trying to spare him, though she supposed that he was still suffering in silence, just as she did. At breakfast this morning, they had scarcely exchanged a word again. After keeping his eyes on his plate of kedgeree, then focussing on the buttering of his toast, as if the mastery of it was the most complicated thing in the world, he had hidden behind his newspaper, until the time came to set out for the factory, when he had awkwardly brushed the top of her head with a kiss and remarked gruffly that it was another bitterly cold day.

Since his departure she had been unable to settle to anything. It would be even worse tomorrow, she thought. The hour set was nine o'clock. She had heard that there was to be a service at the Mission Hall in Huddersfield, led by Reverend Spencer. Ernest's family would be there and some of his friends, praying for him at the end. Florence thought that perhaps she would go to church quietly herself, later in the day, after it was over. Not today though. She did not want to risk leaving the house today, in case word came for her to go to the prison. If not that, then perhaps there would be a letter for her. She pictured Ernest as she had often done in the last few days, standing framed in the prison doorway. Had she just imagined that look of sympathy in his eyes? Or had that momentary sense of a connection been merely her own fancy?

Unusually, the telephone had already rung twice that morning, but the calls had both represented routine household matters: each insistent summons of the bell making her heart race all for nothing. First post had brought her only a dressmaker's bill and a postcard from a friend, who was staying with relatives in Edinburgh. There was still another delivery to come. If Ernest had written to her and his letter had made the early morning post in Leeds, it would surely be through the letter box by tea time.

Though she could not possibly have explained why, and in spite of the fact that he had never sent her a letter before, Florence suddenly felt sure that Ernest was going to write to her, before the end.

CHAPTER TWENTY EIGHT

His Majesty's Prison, Armley, Leeds, Yorkshire
5 February 1934

Dear Miss Morton,

I asked permission for you to visit me today, but as that is not possible, I am writing to you instead. Last time you came here, you asked me to tell you the truth and said that I was holding something back. You were right about that. I have decided that you have a right to know what happened that night and I don't want to die with a lot of lies on my conscience.

When I came back from Greetland that evening, with the cow that wasn't wanted, I dropped my friend, Mr Wright, at his pub in Tadcaster, then drove straight home. I drove into the yard and Dolly was standing at the trough, filling up water buckets, just as I always said she was. As I got out of the horsebox, she came across and started to help me with unloading the cow. I told her about it's not being wanted, and she started telling me that she'd been swimming at Wetherby, with one of her men friends, but I wasn't interested in all that. I interrupted her and asked where Fred was, and she didn't answer me directly, but instead said why did I want to know or something of the sort, so I told her that I wanted to tell him about the cow, and then I wanted to get finished as soon as possible, because I wanted to go back into Tadcaster, to meet my friends.

She said, 'Oh, do you?' a bit sarcastic like.

We'd got the cow across into the mistal by then and I was tethering the beast, when she said, 'Freddie's in the garage. I shot him, when he came home just now.'

She had talked about getting him out of the way before, and it was silly talk like that which had caused me to leave in June, only that time she had persuaded me to come back and said that she had only been joking. She'd promised that there'd be no more of that sort of talk, and that we could remain just friends, if I came back. So when she came out with it this time, I couldn't tell to start with whether she was serious or not, but her saying it made me mad. I grabbed hold of her by the shoulders and asked her if she was joking and she said, 'No. I heard the car coming down the drive and I was waiting for him. Freddie's still in the car, in the garage, and the shot gun is in the wash house.' I'd still got hold of her and when she said that, I shook her and she fell on the floor.

I'd never handled her roughly before and it made her angry. I hadn't intended for her to go down and I reached out a hand to help her up, but she didn't take it. She got up by herself and said: 'You have just done something you will be sorry for.' Then she walked out into the yard, furious like, and called out for Ann and I heard the girl answer her almost straight away.

I could hardly start asking her about Fred with Ann there, so I got some hay for the cow and then I went round to the garage to see if it was really true, and there was your brother, slumped in the driver's seat of the car. I could see right off that he was dead, and if it's any comfort, I think it must have been quick and him not suffering.

Then I went and checked in the wash house and there was the gun, just as she had said. I didn't know what to do. I thought of ringing for the police, there and then, but I could already see that I was in a funny position. There was Dolly, cool as a cucumber and capable of saying anything. I decided the best thing was to ask her what she intended to do, so I went into the kitchen to find her, but there was only Ann Houseman in the room and she said Dolly was upstairs. It was obvious that the girl didn't know anything was amiss, because she was boiling up fruit and sugar in a big pan, humming to herself, just like it was any old evening.

I asked her to fetch Dolly and she went upstairs and then came back to say that Dolly would be down in a minute. Of course I needed to speak to Dolly on her own, as she knew perfectly well, but she was still mad with me for laying hands on her, so she played me up and made me stand there and tell her all about the cow, which she already knew about, because I'd told her about bringing it back, when we were first out in the yard.

I didn't know what to do next, so I went back outside to do my chores. Whatever else has happened, the usual jobs have still got to be done and I thought that Dolly would calm down and come outside to talk with me where we couldn't be overheard. She generally came out of her own accord to help put the ducks away for the night, but when she didn't come, I went in and asked her to help me. Of course I still couldn't say anything to her, because Ann Houseman was there and instead of coming outside, Dolly came up with some excuse about waiting for a telephone call, so I went out again and got on with the job myself. I didn't know at the time whether she was really waiting on a call, or if she was just avoiding having to talk with me. I was thinking that by now, perhaps she'd had time to realise what she had done, and was afraid of the consequences.

I was supposed to have been going back to Tadcaster, for I'd promised Mrs Littlewood a lift, but as you can guess, Mrs Littlewood went straight out of my head with this other business going on, and when I was asked about it later, I had to make up some stuff about it not being a definite arrangement and missing the bus, because otherwise I'd have had to explain why I had forgotten all about Mrs Littlewood, and I couldn't do that.

I kept on going back into the kitchen, but young Ann was always in there, so I couldn't say anything. It occurred to me that one way or another, it wasn't a good thing to have that shotgun lying in the wash house with one live cartridge still in it, so at about half past nine, when it was getting dusk, I took the gun and loosed it off in the yard. I was desperate to talk to Dolly by then and I thought that hearing the shot might bring her to her senses, but when I went back into the kitchen, instead of Dolly there was only Ann Housman there, all wide eyed, and asking what the firing was, so I told her that I'd shot at a rat and went back out again.

No sooner had I gone back outside than there was Dolly, beckoning me round the corner of the house. She'd slipped out by the drawing room window. As you probably remember, there was mud found on the cushions of the window seat, and I guess that got there when Dolly was going in and out.

'You mustn't say anything,' she said to me. 'You have to help me, for the sake of the child.' She meant Baby Diana, who she'd always said was mine. 'What would become of the child?' she said. 'If anything were to happen to me? You would not be able to take her.'

I remember, I just looked at her. She was pleading with me. She kept on saying, 'You have to help me.'

In the end, I agreed to help her for the sake of the child. Bairns are so precious. I've buried a few of my own, so I should know. Please try to understand the position I was in, Miss Morton. Nothing that I could do would alter the fact that Fred was gone and anyway I was hardly thinking straight. I had seen his body, lying there in the car, but I still couldn't believe it was really happening.

'We can pretend it was an accident,' she said. 'You get the gun back into the cupboard. Later on, when Ann and I have gone to bed, you must set fire to the garage. Once the body's burned, no one will know what really happened.'

Thinking about it since, I reckon she'd got it all planned out from the very beginning.

I said, 'I can't do that. It's bloody arson, that is, and what about the stock and all?'

'We can let them out. None of the animals will come to any harm if we're quick about it. I will stay awake and come out to help as soon as you give the alarm,' she said.

'A man can end up doing time in prison for stunts like this,' I said.

'You'll be all right,' she said. 'They've got nothing on you. Everyone will think it's an accident. We'll both tell them about Freddie coming back drunk sometimes, and sleeping it off down in the garage. And don't you think that I will see to it that you are all right? There isn't a magistrate in the district that I'm not on good terms with.'

'No,' I said. 'You just hang on a minute.' I wanted her to wait, but she was off again round the side of the house, before I had time to say anything more, and anyway, I thought I could hear that a horse had got loose, so I went back to the stables to see what was up.

What with seeing to the horse, and fetching down another harness and all, I never heard the phone ring. I saw Dolly and the young woman dashing across the hall, looking all stirred up, but I paid them no mind, until I went back inside with the gun. So far as that was concerned, I didn't mind cleaning it and putting it away, because there's no crime in that, is there?

When I sat down in the kitchen with the gun, I made it clear that I wanted to speak to Dolly on her own, but that Ann girl wouldn't go. I never realised until afterwards that Dolly had probably told her not to. Both myself and Dolly were on edge and the girl must have seen that there was something going on by then, but of course she didn't know what, and afterwards it would have been easy for Dolly to work on her I should imagine, and to get things all twisted around in her mind. They both carried on living under the same roof right up until the trial, so there would have been plenty of chance to talk together and get their story straight, so to speak. I daresay that I did look a bit mad, or wild at times that night, because it's not every day you've a body out in the garage and there's someone trying to embroil you in a mad scheme to get rid of it.

At the trial, the silly young thing even said that she and Dolly had been together the whole time, but that can't have been right, because Dolly came outside and talked to me when she told young Ann that she'd been hiding under the dining room table, and at some point, someone took a knife to those telephone wires, and that wasn't me. I suppose Dolly did it, because she was afraid of someone taking it into their head to phone the police and get them there before the garage went up in flames and poor Fred's body was destroyed.

It would have been easy for Dolly to have taken the knife out of the drawer when the girl wasn't looking, but it was probably more risky to try and smuggle it back inside again, so I suppose that's why she left it out in the barrow in the yard, where it was found next day.

At one time she said to me, pointed like, that someone had called on the telephone, but if she was hinting that it might give Ann Houseman ideas about calling out on it, then I didn't grasp her meaning, which I suppose is why she had to take care of the telephone wires herself.

At about half past ten, I said that I was going to put the Essex away, and I went outside, but I didn't move the car just then. To be honest, I lost my nerve. Something in me didn't want to go down to the garage, and so long as I didn't go down there, then if the police or anyone did turn up, I thought that I could still pretend not to know that Fred was in there. All through the evening, Dolly had kept up this pretence that she was expecting Fred home any minute, and that she couldn't think where he'd got to, and so on and so forth, and I'd gone along with her, because if anyone had come and found that he'd been there all along, I could just say that I hadn't realised that he'd come back.

After the police got involved they tried to find out where he'd been later that evening, after he left the Boot and Shoe, supposedly at about quarter to nine. They never seemed to think of him being there in the garage all along. What must really have happened is that he left Ma Jackson's pub at seven o'clock, as she always said he did, then drove straight to the Boot and Shoe. It's only a couple of minutes between the two. Frank Cawood admitted at the trial that he didn't really know what time it was when Fred came in, nor when he left, and the fact is that he must have arrived home at about ten to eight, while Ann Houseman was out on an errand and I was still on my way back from Greetland. The reason no one heard that first shot is that there was no one but Fred and Dolly there when the gun was fired, and by the time myself and Ann got home, Fred was already dead.

Anyway, I didn't put the Essex away, I went to my hut and sat on the bed for a bit, trying to think things out. I still couldn't decide what to do for the best, so I went back to the kitchen and the three of us carried on like there was nothing unusual going on, and I kept on hoping and hoping that Ann Houseman would go up to bed, so that I could talk to Dolly on her own. I was thinking that maybe I could get her to see reason – to call the police in, but perhaps tell them that there had been some sort of accident, with Fred getting shot by mistake, but then I could see as how that wouldn't work, because of the lies that had already been told in front of Ann Houseman.

Two or three times I signalled to Dolly to send the lass up to bed, but of course Dolly took no notice. I even brought the dog into the kitchen, because I knew that Ann was scared of that big dog, but she still stuck to Dolly like glue. At half past eleven, I went outside and rolled the Essex down to the garage, without turning on the engine. I was hoping that they wouldn't have heard it in the kitchen, as without the engine it's only tyres on the gravel, and of course I'd supposedly put it down in the garage a good half hour or so beforehand, but of course they did hear it and when I came back into the kitchen, Dolly said, cheeky as you like, 'Was that Mr Morton?'

I guessed what she wanted me to do, so I said, 'Yes, but he's going out again.' It was a daft thing to say, but on the spur of the moment it was the only excuse I could think of for why he wouldn't come bowling into the kitchen any minute.

Not long afterwards, I went outside again to stoke up the boiler and when I came back into the kitchen, I found that both the women had gone upstairs. I'd seen Dolly looking out of the bathroom window, so I knew that she had seen me come in. I waited in the kitchen for a while, but she didn't come downstairs, so eventually I went back to my hut and lay on my bed without getting undressed, wondering what I should do. I never went back into the house again that night, whatever silly ideas Dolly may have put into Ann Houseman's head.

Eventually, I decided to do what she'd asked. I couldn't bring your brother back to life and though I was angry with Dolly, I didn't see as there was anything to be gained from my little girl losing both Fred and her mother, and maybe being brought up by folk that didn't really love or care for her as a mother would. In the early hours, when I was sure that the two women would be asleep, I slipped out to the garage, unscrewed the petrol tanks so that the fuel all drained onto the garage floor and then I set the place alight. I went back to my hut and gave it a few minutes to get going, because I knew that as soon as the horses caught a whiff of the smoke, they would start to stamp and call, and I was going to say that that's what woke me, but even before that happened, something gave a bang, so I was able to blame that for waking me instead.

I shouted to raise the household like we'd agreed, but little did I know, they had been awake all along. I was expecting Dolly to come and help with the animals as she'd promised, but there was no sign of her, so I got all the stock out by myself and then I went into the house and tried the telephone, but I couldn't get through. If I had known it was only because the wires to the house were cut, I would have got the key to the office and telephoned the fire brigade from there, but of course I didn't know anything about the wires being cut just then.

Taking a knife to those wires was a damn silly thing to do, because there was no way that could have happened accidentally, and even if the pellets in Fred's body hadn't survived as they did, it would have been obvious that skulduggery was afoot, the minute someone noticed those damaged wires.

Next time I saw Dolly she was on the drive of the house, and of course she was playing her part, giving out orders about fighting the fire and so on. There was PC Broadhead and Murray Stuart and a whole crowd of people dashing about all over the place and so it wasn't until next morning at about half past nine, that she was able to speak with me privately on my own again.

'They're all saying it was an accident,' she said. She seemed really pleased with herself. 'You just stick to knowing nothing, and I'll see you're all right. They can't touch you for anything,' she said. Just then your father's motor car turned in at the gate and her expression turned vexed. 'Damn,' she said. 'I wish they hadn't seen us talking together like this.'

I couldn't understand what was bothering her as there was nothing odd about her being seen talking to an employee on her own the drive. Anyway, I could see she didn't want me there, so I went off and got busy elsewhere. Fire or no fire, there was beasts to be fed and all of the usual jobs, to say nothing of the mess that had been made of everything by the fire itself.

PC Broadhead had ridden to the farm on his bike and as soon as he got there, he asked me when I'd first realised that the fire had started and so forth, and I'd given him my story about the noise waking me up, and about getting the stock out and going for help, and he'd seemed satisfied enough, so when the superintendent asked me to go with him to the police station at Tadcaster the next day to make a statement, I thought they just wanted to know more about how the fire had started, and with me living on the premises, I was the natural person to ask. I was shocked when they arrested me for murdering Fred, but I did as I'd promised Dolly and stuck to my story, and of course, you know the rest.

At the trial, I could hardly believe some of the things Dolly said, but though it upset me, I still didn't think I would be found guilty of something that I hadn't done, and I kept my promise to say nothing for the sake of the child.

A pal of mine what was in Leeds Town Hall on the last day of the trial was standing close by where Dolly and her father were sitting, when word of the verdict reached them. He told me that she showed nothing at all, when she heard it. 'You might have been a complete stranger that she'd never even met, for all the notice she took,' he said.

I have told the governor all of this today and written some of it down for him, though in not so much detail as I have to you, because he was in a hurry to catch the London train. He seems to think that it might make a difference to what happens, but I think it is probably too late now.

I don't suppose you will receive this letter until tomorrow, but at least now you will know all of it Miss Morton, and will be able to tell your father too. It upset me to think that he would believe it was me that done it, because he recommended me to Fred and always thought well of me until now. I also told my mother and sister the truth of it all, when they came to see me for the last time, this afternoon.(I have told them too of the way you have come to visit me and signed the petition and written a letter and all, and they think very well of you and thank you for it.)

Thank you again for coming to see me, and I hope you will join my family in saying a prayer for me.

Yours faithfully

Ernest Brown

CHAPTER TWENTY NINE

Monday 5 February 1934
The Home Office, Whitehall, London

'Well gentlemen, I must say that this is a singular state of affairs.'

In spite of its being a strictly informal meeting, the Director of Public Prosecutions, Sir Edward Tindal Atkinson, had naturally assumed leadership of the trio. After an indifferent lunch of Brown Windsor soup, roast leg of lamb and apple pie, Tindal Atkinson, together with Mr Paley Scott, and Mr Welsby his junior counsel, had been ushered to a small private sitting room which had been set aside for their deliberations, and handed them the thin brown envelope conveyed in such haste from Leeds.

The meal had been a convivial affair, not in the least overshadowed by the serious deliberations which they were about to undertake, their conversation laced with anecdotes of a humorous nature and gossip regarding various friends and rivals at the top of the profession, for Sir Edward was good company, in spite of his turned down mouth and almost constant expression of melancholy. Mindful of the staff who waited at table and their instructions to maintain the highest levels of confidentiality, the three men had steered the conversation well away from anything even remotely connected to the Morton murder case, and only now that they were alone, with the slender, plain brown envelope containing no more than a dozen sheets of foolscap paper, did their talk turn to the reason which had unexpectedly brought them together.

'It is of course highly unusual to take into account something which has appeared so very late in the day and has not been subjected to the full scrutiny of proper court proceedings,' Sir Edward continued. 'Of course, we must not forget that a man's life hangs in the balance here and that we are all instruments in the process of justice. We must also bear in mind that it is extremely dangerous to even consider overturning a legal verdict, which has been properly arrived at, after due process has been followed. To undertake such a course would undoubtedly lead many people to question the validity of the original verdict, and quite possibly shake the confidence of the general public in the normal legal system, and such a course should therefore not be embarked upon lightly. As we know only too well, there are always a minority of agitators who like nothing better than to seize upon the slightest doubt in any case, in order to further their own agenda.'

'Indeed yes.' Mr Paley Scott nodded. 'Not for nothing has it sometimes been said that it may be better for the occasional innocent man to languish in jail, than for the whole edifice of British justice to be called into question.'

'I have to say,' the Director of Public Prosecutions continued, 'that although my opinion in this matter has been sought, I feel that I know relatively little of the case, save what I remember reading in briefings at the time – as you may recall, for various reasons, I was not directly involved and of course, time has passed and one does not memorise every detail. There is obviously no time for a full re-reading of the evidence given at trial, as Sir John Gilmour requires an answer from us this afternoon, and I will therefore be forced to rely heavily upon you gentlemen for guidance.'

Mr Paley Scott made a mental note that the rumours he had heard about Tindal Atkinson were evidently true. He had never sought the office which he now occupied and had gained a reputation as a man whose main preoccupation was not to be wrong-footed. Aloud he said, 'While I obviously recall a good deal about the matter, and I have brought with me the notes which I made at the time in order to aid my examination and summing up, I have to confess that some of the finer points of detail may now escape me. It is almost two months since I have had to fully focus on the case and I have of course read numerous other briefs since then.'

'Of course, of course.' Tindal Atkinson nodded sympathetically. 'We can only endeavour to do our best in the somewhat trying circumstances with which we are confronted.'

'I gather that there is no question of postponing the execution in order to give us a little more time.' Mr Welsby, the most junior member of the gathering put in.

'There is no possibility of that,' said Sir Edward firmly. 'The date has already been put back twice, amid much protest, and if it were to be put back again there would have to be some public explanation given out for this further delay and the Home Secretary naturally does not want to go down that road.'

'Of course not.' Mr Paley Scott's tone was brisk. 'After all, we don't want every condemned man perpetually delaying the business by coming up with a different story at the last minute. In addition I regret to say that I cannot devote the entire day to the problem, as I have a pressing engagement at four thirty this afternoon.'

'I am sure this the matter is not going to detain us overlong,' said Tindal Atkinson. 'The new account of the affair appears to be quite brief.'

'I imagine it was composed in some haste,' said Mr Welsby. 'From what I have been told, the prisoner was only given a very limited time to produce something on paper.'

'Well obviously. At least it will be in the fellow's own words, and not translated into police-ese,' remarked Mr Paley Scott. 'I was proceeding in a south easterly direction along the highway, and all that kind of nonsense.'

'Before we actually turn our attention to reading what the man has to say, perhaps you gentlemen could give me your opinion of him – as a man?' suggested the DPP.

'Certainly.' Paley Scott jumped in immediately. 'From official records he emerged as something of a bad lot. In his youth he'd been birched for theft and later on he appeared several times in the police courts for being drunk and disorderly.'

'Nothing of a criminal nature in more recent years?'

'No. Though he had also deserted from the army towards the end of his service.'

'That would also have been some years ago, I suppose?'

'About 1919 from what I can remember.'

'What of his general demeanour?'

'Insolent sort of fellow, I thought. It appeared that the victim, Frederick Morton, thought pretty well of him, but there – all the while he was enjoying the fellow's company in the local pub, the chap was making free with Morton's wife, behind his back.'

Sir Edward laughed. 'It doesn't sound as if Mr Frederick Morton was a terribly good judge of character does it?'

'Neither in his choice of servants, nor in his choice of wife,' quipped Welsby and all three men laughed again.

'So essentially we are not really talking about a man who might well agree to tell lies at his own cost, in order to protect a lady's honour, eh?'

'If you mean, Sir Edward, is Ernest Brown an officer and a gentleman, then I think the answer is without a doubt that he is not.'

'Very well then, with this in mind, let us see what he has to say.'

The room fell silent as each of them turned their attention to the statement provided by the prisoner. It had been typed up in the governor's office by John Wilton, prior to the governor catching the train to London. Sir Edward Tindal Atkinson had the benefit of the original, while the other two men made do with carbon copies, which had been made with slightly smudgy purple ink and produced on tissue thin, flimsy paper, which whispered in protest at the slightest touch.

It was not a long document. As they had rightly surmised, Ernest Brown had been working very much against the clock to produce it, and it contained only the bare bones of his story.

'You know the case better than I, of course,' Tindal Atkinson said, when it was clear that all three men had finished reading. 'But it seems somewhat preposterous that a lady like Mrs Morton – for all that she is a somewhat flighty woman – would go about cutting her own telephone wires, still less shooting her husband for apparently no reason at all. It makes the woman sound as if she's off her head. She's not, I suppose?' he added, by way of an afterthought.

'On the contrary, Mrs Morton always appeared to be an extremely level headed woman. She showed great composure throughout.'

'If I may put in a word,' said Mr Welsby. 'It seems to me that certain fundamental points should not be ignored. Frederick Morton was shot and the only person seen handling a gun at the farm that night was Ernest Brown. The telephone wires were sawed apart with a knife, and again we find Ernest Brown taking a knife outside at the vital time when this must have occurred. Finally the garage was set alight at a time when Mrs Morton and her companion had each other in plain view. Again this can only have been the act of Ernest Brown.'

'Unless you believe Mr Streatfield's theory of a phantom lover,' Paley Scott put in with a chuckle.

'Phantom lover?' queried Tindal Atkinson.

'Just a desperate idea thrown into the melting pot by the defence counsel.'

'Oh, I see,' said the DPP, who didn't, but decided that it was better to let the point go.

'There is also the testimony of Mrs Morton's companion,' Mr Welsby said. 'It appears to corroborate Mrs Morton and thoroughly incriminate Brown. There is no suggestion in this new story that she was in some way complicit in the murder, and she had no motive whatsoever to involve herself in the murder of her employer. What reason had the girl to lie?'

'For me,' said Paley Scott, 'the biggest single problem with Brown's latest story is that Frederick Morton cannot possibly have been lying dead at Saxton Grange when Brown arrived there at a quarter past eight, because the man was seen arriving at a public house in Peckfield at precisely the same time. I have it here in my notes,' he flicked through until he found the relevant page, then read aloud: 'Cawood of the Boot and Shoe Inn testified that Frederick Morton arrived at the Boot and Shoe at around quarter past eight and left there about half an hour later. If that is correct, then Brown cannot possibly be telling the truth.'

'The witness only estimated the time, but a witness is hardly going to be a whole hour out,' Welsby put in. 'And while one can believe that Brown might have initially lied in order to protect Mrs Morton, it is hardly likely that a man of his type would go on doing so, even to the point of being executed for a crime he did not commit.'

'Gentlemen,' said Sir Edward. 'I hardly think we need to detain ourselves any longer over this matter. I suggest that since you have a pressing engagement Mr Paley Scott, I will convey our unanimous views to Sir John Gilmour in person. I am sure that I can speak for the Home Secretary in thanking you both for your valuable time.'

CHAPTER THIRTY

Tuesday 6 February 1934
His Majesty's Prison, Armley, Yorkshire

It seemed to John Wilton that the tension which had infused the entire prison in the hours before, during and after the execution, still hung heavily upon the governor himself. It would not have been fitting of course, for Wilton to have asked anything about what had taken place, during Ernest Brown's last moments. He knew that it was a long walk between the condemned cell and the place of execution. Someone had once told him that the walk at Armley was the longest in the country. As the man who dealt with all the governor's correspondence, he was aware that there were plans afoot to install new, modern execution facilities in all the country's prisons, which would remove the necessity for the prisoner to walk more than a few feet before he came face to face with the noose, but there were no such arrangements in place at Armley yet.

Wilton had not been in post long enough to know precisely what delicate protocol ought to be observed in the aftermath of an execution, but he did know that the various contents of the manila folder on his desk had to be attended to by the governor himself, and that because there were some personal letters from the prisoner involved, there could not be any undue delay.

The execution had been over for a couple of hours now. Ernest Brown had been officially certified dead, the governor had bid farewell to the various dignitaries whose duty had brought them there this morning, and had his usual morning tea and biscuits brought in at eleven o'clock. Wilton decided that the moment was right. He rose from his desk, collecting up the folder as he did so, walked the four steps across the red and black carpet which took him to his customary position, immediately in front of his boss's desk, and said, 'I have the last letters written by the prisoner Brown here sir, and also one written to Brown's parents from the chaplain.'

'Very well, pass them over.' The governor didn't look up as the file was put into his outstretched hand.

Wilton continued to stand before the desk, waiting silently while his boss scrutinised each sheet in turn. Even if he had not already perused them, Wilton could easily have learned their contents, since he numbered among his various talents, the ability to read handwriting from upside down.

The uppermost piece of correspondence was the lengthy letter which the prisoner had written to Miss Florence Morton, the day before. Though he must have guessed the contents, the governor took enough time to read it all the way through, before putting it to one side and saying, without raising his head, 'Obviously this cannot possibly go any further. As we learned from the Thorne case, and others before it, letters such as these always find their way into the newspapers, and the service doesn't exist to give guilty men a platform for publicity – not even posthumous publicity.'

Wilton said nothing. He was well aware of the regulations, and had guessed the moment he began to read it, that the letter to Miss Morton would never be sent, but censorship of a prisoner's final correspondence was always a matter for the governor himself.

'Hmm.' The governor glanced through the second letter, which was addressed to Brown's mother and was much shorter. 'Mostly domestic matters, asking her to take good care of his little daughter and to make sure that a small loan from one of his friend's gets repaid – strange how a tiny debt can play on a man's mind at such a time. What a pity he mentions that he has written to Miss Morton. Well, we obviously can't let that one go either, Wilton, as it gives away the existence of this other letter, I'm afraid.'

So saying he laid the letter to Brown's mother on top of the one to Florence.

'Now then, what does the padre have to say?' It was a rhetorical question. The governor was already beginning to read it as he spoke.

Dear Mrs Brown,

The last thing Ernest asked me to do was write to you. He sends his love and asks especially about his daughter.

I trust it will be a comfort to you to know that we prayed together and that he found peace with God and prayed for you all. The last words I read to him were from Psalm 46, The Lord is our refuge and our strength, a very present help in trouble. Therefore we will not fear.

I send you my sincere sympathy and my prayers.

Yours sincerely

Reverend George Hadfield

The governor hesitated and sighed. 'Oh dear,' he said. 'Reverend Hadfield really ought to know better. It is not the role of the prison service to sympathise with the family of a convicted man. Expressions of sympathy in respect of a man convicted of a brutal murder are wholly inappropriate. Keep it in the file with the others.'

'Yes, sir.'

Wilton watched as the governor squared the papers against the solid surface of his desk and replaced them in their manila cover. He reached out at the appropriate moment to take the folder back. As he returned to his desk, he found that the blotter, pen and inkstand had become unaccountably blurred. It was no secret that Reverend Hadfield – even without the benefit of seeing Brown's final version of what had taken place – had come to believe that the man was innocent. But whether the condemned man was guilty or not, Wilton thought, what had his poor family done to be denied whatever little bit of comfort such a letter might bring?

CHAPTER THIRTY ONE

Martin's Nest
Holywell Green
Yorkshire
7 February 1934
To the Home Secretary.

Dear Sir,

I am writing to you regarding Ernest Brown, who was executed yesterday after being found guilty of the murder of my brother Frederick Morton. My father and I continue to be deeply troubled about this matter and it would greatly put our minds at rest to know whether or not Ernest Brown made some kind of additional statement or confession before he died. I would be most grateful for any information you are able to provide for us.

Yours sincerely

Florence Ellison Morton

The Office of the Home Secretary
Whitehall
London
8 February 1934

Dear Miss Morton,

The Home Secretary has asked me to write and inform you that he has been in contact with His Majesty's Prison, Armley and is able to confirm that Ernest Brown made no final confession or statement regarding the circumstances of the crime.

The Home Secretary asks me to again offer his condolences on your loss.

Yours sincerely

Charles Featherstone

On behalf of Sir John Gilmour – Home Secretary.

CHAPTER THIRTY TWO

Monday 19 February 1934
Martin's Nest, Holywell Green, Yorkshire

Florence was deeply engrossed in the household accounts when she heard the thud thud of the front door knocker. Bother! Who on earth could it be at this time of day? Not a tradesman, who would surely have gone round to approach cook at the back door, and it would hardly be someone paying calls, as it was far too early in the day for that. It was bound to be some tiresome interruption that she could very well do without. She glanced out of the morning room window, but there was no sign of a motor car at the front of the house. Oh well, Hilda or Grace would answer it and let her know who was there soon enough.

In fact it was several minutes before there was a tap on the door, followed by the appearance of Hilda, who rather than remaining in the doorway, entered the room and closed the door behind her in a somewhat conspiratorial fashion.

'Begging your pardon, Miss Florence, but there's some women outside, asking if they might see you.'

'Don't you mean ladies, Hilda?'

'No mum. I don't.' Hilda was defensive yet emphatic. 'They say their names are Brown, mum. Mrs Brown and Miss Doris Brown.' She dropped her voice and added, 'I believe they are the mother and sister of that man who was hanged, mum. Should I send them away?'

'Certainly not. How ever have they got all the way out here? Has someone driven them?'

'No, Miss Florence,' Hilda favoured her mistress with the look which she always used when confronted with what she felt to be a foolish enquiry. 'I 'spect they took the bus and then walked it from the bottom road.'

'Of course, of course. They must be absolutely frozen. Is the fire lit in the drawing room?'

'Yes, Miss Florence.'

'Then show Mrs Brown and her daughter in there. I will come in directly.'

'Into the drawing room, mum?' Hilda made no attempt to disguise her incredulity.

'Yes, Hilda,' Florence said very firmly. 'Show them into the drawing room and then kindly bring in some tea – and… and some cakes or biscuits, or something, whatever cook has to hand.'

It was the toss of the head as Hilda departed that did it. I'm giving that girl notice at the end of the month, Florence decided, as she swiftly checked that the cap was back on her pen, and from force of habit patted her hair into place.

She crossed the hall to the drawing room, where she found the two women standing awkwardly on the central rug, no doubt very conscious of the house parlour maid's reluctant welcome, which had probably been accompanied by a pointed up and down look at their rather shabby winter coats and worn out shoes. It was strange, Florence had often thought, the way that snobbery was at its sharpest among the servant class. If Florence in any way noticed how out of place the two women looked in the drawing room, she gave no sign, instead approaching each in turn and giving their hands a welcoming squeeze.

'Thank you for coming all this way,' she said. 'Please do sit down near the fire. I think you must have come to tell me something about Ernest – perhaps something that he told you at the very end?'

A POSTSCRIPT FROM THE AUTHOR

Many readers will be surprised by the somewhat bleak ending to this novel. If this story had been entirely fictional, there would surely have been a last minute reprieve and Ernest Brown would not have been hanged. A really ambitious (and particularly unrealistic) author might have engineered a scenario in which it was Florence Morton herself who somehow effected his acquittal and release. She would have been there to meet him at the prison gates when he emerged, blinking, from Armley jail. They would have got into her waiting motor car together, with more than a hint of romance in the air. But this story is based on fact and though a substantial degree of poetic licence has been employed in respect of characterisations and dialogue, with some minor characters invented and events sometimes compressed or slightly adjusted for the sake of clarity, the basic facts have not been altered. Ernest Brown was convicted of the murder of Frederick Morton and after a failed appeal, a considerable public campaign, and even a last minute dash down to London by the prison governor on the eve of the execution, on 6 February 1934 Ernest Brown paid the ultimate price which the law then exacted for the crime of murder.

It is a matter of historical record that Florence Morton did not believe that the full facts regarding her brother's death had come out at Brown's trial, that she visited Ernest Brown on at least two occasions between the trial itself and his execution, that she wrote to the Home Secretary expressing her concerns, and that she joined well over 9,000 other people in signing a petition which sought to have Brown's sentence commuted.

The evidence of the witnesses (both those heard at the trial and those who were not heard) which appears in this novel, closely follows the contemporary records, and it is a fact that on the day prior to his execution, Brown entirely changed his story from the one which he had previously told, stating for the first time that Dorothy Morton had shot her husband and that he had merely assisted her in an attempt to conceal the deed, in order to protect Dorothy herself, and more importantly the child, Diana, whom he believed to be his daughter. His written statement was taken to London in person, by the prison governor, in a last ditch attempt to gain a reprieve, but Brown's new version of events was dismissed as a pack of lies by the assembled legal professionals to whom it was shown.

Some readers may share my own reservations about the propriety of inviting the men whose role had been to prosecute the case against Brown, to form the tribunal which ultimately decided his fate. The notes of their deliberations suggest that they applied a less than open minded approach to this task and it is difficult to understand how they could so easily dismiss Brown's final story, since it explained a number of discrepancies thrown up by the accounts which had been provided by Dorothy Morton and Ann Houseman. It is extremely telling that this trio of highly intelligent men elected to rely on an estimated time, when considering the evidence regarding Frederick Morton's visit to the inn at Peckfield. It had emerged clearly at the trial that the witness Francis Cawood was not at all sure of the time that night, and his estimate made no sense at all when placed alongside the testimony of Maria Jackson, but in spite of this, Mr Paley Scott and co. decided that Cawood's evidence disproved Ernest Brown's story. There are none so blind as those who will not see...

After writing his new statement for the governor, Brown also wrote a last letter to Florence Morton, telling her the truth about what had happened, but the letter was suppressed, as were his final letter to his mother, and a letter to his parents from the prison chaplain. For the purposes of this novel, I have altered the wording of the letters, but maintained the spirit of them. The original correspondence survives in its entirety in the Home Office files relating to the case, which are housed in the National Archives. In line with government policy on archival material, these files were originally the subject of a 75 year closure rule, and were therefore scheduled to remain closed until 2007, however like many old criminal cases, the files were later subject to a policy of accelerated opening, and their contents were therefore freely available for many years, to anyone who obtained a reader's ticket. In 2014 staff at the National Archives decided to withdraw the files under their Takedown and Review Policy, and at the time of writing in 2018 the files remain closed, pending a decision on whether or not their contents are suitable for the general public. It goes without saying that as an author and researcher, I deplore the implementation of a closure which is well in excess of that originally envisaged, especially given that none of the original participants in this drama are still living and that the only readers whose sensitivities are likely to be offended by the contents, are those who have a sense of justice.

Somewhat ironically, the Saxton Grange murder has been remembered – if at all – firstly for the remarkable survival of the one part of the victim's body which contained irrefutable evidence that Frederick Morton's death was no accident, and secondly for its supposed connection with the 1931 murder of Evelyn Foster.

Anyone who researches both cases will quickly realise that the alleged connection is entirely spurious. It seems to have originated in a claim that immediately prior to his execution, Brown uttered the words, 'Ought to burn' or 'Otterburn' – a suggestion which cannot be traced any further back than an account of the Foster murder produced by the late Jonathan Goodman in 1977. There is no evidence whatsoever in the case files to support the idea that Brown said this or indeed anything like it, either on the scaffold or elsewhere, or that he had anything at all to do with the murder of Evelyn Foster, but unfortunately Goodman's story continues to be repeated in various articles and on the internet.

In a lifetime of reading about famous cases from the 1930s, I had never encountered any suggestion that the verdict against Ernest Brown was even controversial, still less that it probably represented a miscarriage of justice, and I was therefore astonished when I finally read the contents of the case files, and discovered the hitherto unsuspected information which they contained.

The prison governor's notes record that on the eve of his execution, when Brown finally changed his story to implicate Dorothy Morton, the governor asked Ernest Brown why he had not told the truth in the first place. Brown replied that he had not believed that he could be found guilty, partly because the evidence against him was only circumstantial, but principally because he believed that since he was an innocent man, the jury could not possibly find him guilty *beyond reasonable doubt.* Brown was by no means the first or last man accused of a serious crime, who imagined that the fact of his innocence would in itself provide absolute protection, and that he could therefore get away with telling lies in court. Put simply, Ernest Brown did not believe that the British justice system was capable of convicting an innocent man.

I have ended this novel by bringing together Ernest Brown's mother – to whom, during her last visit on the eve of his execution, he had given a verbal account of what he says actually happened at Saxton Grange on that fateful day in September 1933 – and Florence Morton, whose attempts to obtain the letter which she evidently suspected that Ernest Brown had written to her, were met with a lie by the Home Office.

In fiction therefore, Florence Morton – a courageous heroine, who at a time when young, unmarried woman were expected to do as they were told, was prepared to stand out against convention in the face of a perceived injustice – gets a form of closure. Regrettably there is no evidence that this meeting between herself and the women of Ernest Brown's family, ever took place in real life.

Diane Janes
October 2018